SLAVE REVOLT...

It was impossible to flick the pistol out of the white man's hand as it was raised toward Sebastian. There was too much space between them.

It was Grace who saved him for the moment, perhaps without meaning to, but possibly on purpose. She had been swaying back and forth, badly wounded. Now she fell, her body descending on the exposed lantern flame. For a moment the room was again smothered by darkness. Sebastian ducked and swerved out of the path of danger even as the pistol exploded one more time.

As he moved, safe for the moment, Sebastian knew that the odor of burning flesh had been added to the others in the suffocating room. Grace's body was on fire . . .

SEBASTIAN

by

Lionel Webb

WILDSIDE PRESS

Chapter One

Waiting, his hands on the frayed tophat that he would be wearing on stage, Sebastian was distracted by a sound backstage. Somebody was walking heavily in the thick boots that men wore this year—1847— walking so heavily that the sound might carry past the stage and into the audience.

Without thinking, Sebastian whirled and drew a hard, heavy finger to his painted lips.

The white man, stomping as if he owned the theatre as well as the entire state of Georgia, stopped and stared at the sight of a made-up Negro with a tophat in hand.

"I'll be damned," he got out thickly. "A play-acting Negro. If that isn't the damnedest thing I ever saw in my whole life, I don't know what is."

Sebastian grew rigid, but he said quietly, "Keep it down or the people will hear you."

"You trying to give me orders, nigger?" the white man flushed. "If I had my riding crop with me, I'd lay one across that disgusting face of yours."

Sebastian looked around for somebody to help him get the chunky white man out of earshot. There wasn't anybody in sight though, and he couldn't walk away. He must have looked at the white man furiously.

The white man suddenly flung out his fists and shouted, "You nigger son of a bitch!"

Sebastian raised both fists and punched the charging white man in the stomach. When the white man was doubled up, his face gray, Sebastian punched him in the mouth. The white man reeled, surprise etched along with murderous anger.

"You giddamn—" he started, bellowing.

Sebastian followed up his advantage, drawing a hand up over the white man's mouth to keep him from calling out and bothering the actors on stage.

7

The chunky white man promptly drew both hands to Sebastian's neck and began to squeeze. Sebastian was sure he could feel the blood leaving his face as well as his heart beating tightly, even feel his feet getting numb.

He took advantage of the man's closeness to him, drawing the man's head back as if he wanted to crack his neck. Part of him was listening for the cue-line; he tried to make up his mind what he'd do if he suddenly heard it.

". . . no, music isn't the food of love, my dear, but food is the music of love," the male actor on stage was saying.

The chunky white man's face showed surprise at resistance from a black. His eyes bulged with fury and he breathed in jagged gasps. Sebastian raised his hand to cover the white man's nostrils and keep him from breathing until the pressure was eased on Sebastian's neck.

The theatre manager, attracted by the noise, hurried over. The manager had spoken hardly a word to Sebastian since the black had become an active part of the First Boston Repertory Company, paying a visit to the Georgia town of Tremont.

Sebastian, head cocked as he listened for his cue, said to the manager, "He tried to keep me from going on."

The boor got his voice back while the manager was nodding. "If this black ain't jailed right away, I'll break him to pieces, I swear I will."

The manager shrugged. "If you go on stage, son, Mr. Crosby over here will probably try and scream my house down."

Sebastian bit his lower lip and nodded sadly.

". . . A woman is as sensitive as an ocelot's claws," the male actor on stage continued.

That was Sebastian's cue. There was no time to arrange for a white man to do his part in blackface.

8

"If you've got the name," he said quietly, "you might as well get the game."

And he rabbit-punched the boorish Crosby, who folded up and closed his eyes as he crumpled. Sebastian watched closely—in case he ever had to play a beaten man on stage—then turned and started for the stage.

The manager caught him. "Now comes the really hard part, boy. There are four hundred whites on the other side of that stage. They're not going to enjoy seeing you out there."

Sebastian hurried on, not knowing whether the owner had wished him good luck.

Grace Parker, sitting in her box at the theatre, glanced to one side and wondered why it was taking Eli Crosby such a long time to get back. Eli had excused himself a little while ago and was nowhere in sight.

Grace was a good-looking girl in her late twenties, wearing red with frilly red lace, all the rage this August. The dress showed off her white skin, heightening it by contrast as well as her swept-back blond hair. She wore her blond hair that way often.

She hadn't been too much younger when she had left her father's plantation, Rootstock, for the "grand tour" of Europe. The tour had come to a dead stop at a French watering place that was the dullest place on Earth. Grace was praying for a chance to leave her companions and get away from Deauville. Her wish was granted, as it happened, but at a terrible cost. A letter had come from her father's lawyer, a letter which let her know that her father had suddenly passed away.

Grace had come back to Tremont and the knowledge that she owned Rootstock. She knew, too, that she could do nothing to keep it up on her own. More and more in these few months she had leaned on the help and advice of a fellow plantation owner, Eli Crosby. It was true that Eli drank more than was good for him, but he helped her considerably in managing Rootstock, for he was hoping that their relationship might one day be much closer.

Not too far from the torchlit stage below her, Grace could hear sounds of a man talking loudly. For a moment she thought that the man was Eli. Perhaps she ought to have gone to look for him.

She was stopped by the sudden silence of the audience. Until that moment they had been friendly, waiting for another chance to laugh. Now they seemed drawn together, and a wave of hatred passed from them to the stage.

An actor had made his entrance, a young fellow in blackface and with a frayed tophat on his head. As soon as the young man spoke everyone knew that he was a black. It seemed that no Negro, Southern or free, could hide for long from crude white hate-mongers.

He seemed to be a handsome young man, moving with a certain smoothness that told he knew exactly what he was doing. Grace relaxed. He would not make of himself a laughingstock.

"The inheritance is yours, little miss," he was saying to the child actress. The audience murmured restlessly at seeing a Negro actor on the same stage with whites. The sounds grew louder.

The child actress looked confused.

Grace Parker, after another look at the handsome young Negro, leaned forward when he had finished one speech and applauded vigorously.

The Negro stepped back, astonished. The child actress, jarred, hesitated before going on. The white man who shared the stage with them darted an angry glance up toward Grace. The play seemed to have come to a stop, but after a minute it went on without any further incident.

10

Eli Crosby was on a couch when he opened his eyes in a room with theatrical posters lining the walls. The theatre manager, whose name was Hobson, approached at the sound of Crosby moving on the couch.

"I'm gonna put that nigra in jail," Crosby said.

"The whole town will know he knocked you out," Hobson remarked.

Eli Crosby's eyes narrowed to slits. "I can just tell the court he tried to attack me. I'll get justice."

"But I myself would have to testify that you were disturbing the actors on stage and that you'd been drinking too much," Hobson said slowly. "I've got some money tied up in these performances, and I don't want no trouble until they're over. I mean that, sir."

Eli Crosby stood up slowly but angrily and walked to the door, keeping his gait steady. In the warm, torchlit Georgia night, he cursed. Carriages and horses with their drivers waited at curbsides. Most of the drivers were Negroes, but with his plantation owner's eye for judging a man's strengths, he thought the driver at the far left might handle the job that Eli Crosby wanted done.

He had taken two steps when a white beggar appeared at his right side, smiling and deferential.

"Could you let me have a little something to feed a starving family, sir?"

"To feed 'em whiskey, I suppose, judging from your breath," Eli Crosby said, careful to look straight ahead of him. "Out of my way, you."

The beggar took a grip on him that became surprisingly strong. "You've got so much, sir, so I'm sure you can spare a little something for those who haven't got anything to speak of."

Eli Crosby turned to him and said quietly, "Take your hand off me and I'll give you a chance to earn the money."

The beggar took his hands away, unhappy at the

11

prospect of work but willing to listen further. He was a young man with a two-day growth of beard and no sideburns.

"You mean for me to take a job?" he asked doubtfully. "How much will you pay?"

"Five dollars for you and five dollars for another strong lad. Can you find one?"

"For five dollars," the beggar said, "I'll find you Samson himself, with all his hair grown back."

"See that you do. I expect you to help take some heavy cargo back to my home with me, back to where I can teach it a good lesson . . . well, never mind. Get busy and bring another lad over here. I haven't got all night to wait."

Sebastian, finished acting for the night, looked pensively at the white actors on their way out to a tavern for drinks and a late meal. Hungry as he might have been, he knew better than to join them.

"The white places won't have you," Mr. Borradaile, the director, had said, "and the colored places are at least as dangerous for you. You're different from the other coloreds, Sebastian, and that makes you a target for them. Best to go to your boarding house and stay there till the morning meeting at the theatre."

He had agreed to do just that.

After taking off his make-up he walked out to the warm Georgia night, hoping to find a horse and carriage.

He hid a smile when a white beggar approached, hand outstretched, to ask for money. Somebody else was walking on the street behind him. He paid no attention as he turned to the white beggar. It afforded him a certain wry satisfaction to be giving money to a white man.

Afterwards, he told himself bitterly that the white man and his accomplice had been counting on that feeling of bitter satisfaction to lull his natural alert-

12

ness. As he drew out a coin and leaned forward to give it to the white beggar, he heard a sudden sound of whistling directly behind him. There was a moment of total blackness, and then he knew nothing.

Sebastian had been born and raised in Boston. His father, whose name was Morny, had been a slave in the Deep South, but had wangled his freedom by promising to pay his former owner a certain amount of money every month. He had then skipped North instead of paying.

Sebastian's mother, Sarah, was a quiet and hard-working woman who supported the family by working for white people. Morny had walked out on his family after a while. Every so often he would mail them a squeezed-up dollar bill or a five or a ten. Whenever a ten dollar bill came along, Sarah would buy her son a suit of clothes.

Sebastian wanted some money of his own. One evening, on the way back from work, Sarah found him in front of the Boston Civic Center. He was opening hansom cabs that pulled up, standing to one side as the white patrons stepped out. Sarah practically dragged him home.

"You made money by kissing the whites you-know-where," Sarah said, "and letting 'em rub your head for good luck. I won't have you waiting on whites."

"But you wait on them," Sebastian said, wounded. "You cook and clean."

"I work for them because I need to do it to keep both of us eating."

He met a girl named Lucinda at about that time, and he needed money more than ever. Lucinda was older than Sebastian, all of sixteen, and she hinted that she knew what was to be known about sex and other such mysteries. Sebastian went to work as best he could, opening cab doors in front of the Civic Center as he had never done before. He wanted

13

enough money so that he could keep inviting Lucinda to go out with him.

"Nothing happens, though," he complained to his best friend, Simon. "She lets me see her up to her door and that's absolutely all."

"It'll happen," Simon told him. "Happened to me with a different gal. They all are aching to do it, you know."

"I've heard that, but I haven't seen it work out," Sebastian snapped. "Besides, she's older than me. Why would she want to do it with me?"

"Gals like to break in younger fellows," Simon said loftily. "It makes 'em feel better. They figure young fellows are more eager for it."

Lucinda decided to reward him one night after a pleasant evening together. Nobody was at home and she took Sebastian into her room. She told him how to undress her, then he shucked his own outfit and got into bed and lay down next to her.

It turned out to be a bad night for him, mainly because Lucinda wanted him to do something to her that he simply didn't want to do. She kept insisting, and the more she insisted the more stubborn he became. Finally, desperate and against her apparent will, he got on top of her. She writhed and bit and kicked, but he quieted her at last. When he tried to find out where to stick part of himself into, he couldn't find the place. It had to be among her hairs and close to the meat of her legs, but he couldn't find it. Then his erection subsided.

Lucinda howled, spurring him to climb off. It was going to be useless without her help, and she wouldn't do anything for him unless he did that particular and dirty thing to her.

He got up from the bed, sick at heart, and walked to his clothes. He had put on the pants up to the ankles when Lucinda reached out a well-formed meaty hand to his manhood and held him lightly by it.

14

Maybe next time we'll know what to do."

He remained so upset that her touch did nothing for him at all. He was chilled to the bone when he left Lucinda's on that warm August evening.

"There ain't nothing wrong with you," Simon told him, for maybe the tenth time. "You didn't feel like doing what she wanted you to do. That's all."

"But I tell you that the thing wouldn't move. It just *sat* there, Simon, small as a pinkie finger. I could'a gone through the floor."

"All right, so for once the hammer didn't strike," Simon said. "That don't mean there's something for you to be ashamed of."

Sebastian didn't believe it, though. He often made things more dramatic than they actually were and told himself he was getting used to the idea that he'd never be able to stick his penis into a woman. When he met Samantha he practically hinted that she shouldn't expect him to be able to do that thing. Samantha, a well-built gal who smiled cheerfully whether there was any reason for it or not, smiled at him again.

"Soon as Samantha gets through with you, boy, you'll be too tired to know if anything got done or it didn't."

She was almost as good as her word, as it happened. She was practically a machine in bed, telling him what to do and how to do it. Meanwhile, she made him feel as if every idea was his own. He had never known such a good time in his life, and made up his mind that he wouldn't spend too many nights away from Samantha, who he'd probably get married up with.

Samantha left Boston in a few weeks, which disappointed Sebastian mightily.

While he was getting better day by day, with

15

school out and nothing to do, Sebastian found out about the theatre. The First Boston Repertory was putting on plays. He went whenever he could. One night Sarah found him posturing in front of the only mirror in their three rooms.

"Oh what a rogue and peasant slave am I," he was declaiming.

"Don't never let me hear you say that part 'bout being a slave," Sarah snapped. "Never—you hear?"

"But it's part of a play, ma. The play I saw today."

"And now you want to become a play-actor, I s'pose." Sarah sniffed. "Well, it's better news than what I figured when I seen you waving 'round in front of the mirror. I thought you'd gone Sandy."

Sandy Field was a little boy with whom Sebastian had grown up, and who now wore gal's clothes when he could get them and told strangers "her" name was Clara.

"I want to be an actor and I can be pretty good at it."

"You're about twenty shades too dark for the job, Sebastian. Maybe thirty shades. It don't matter how good you might be, only what color you are."

"That's wrong," he said fiercely. "I'm going down to that theatre tomorrow morning and you see if they don't put me to work acting right away."

Sarah snorted and walked out. Next morning, Sebastian went down to the Civic Center where the troupe performed. He had to walk around the place for an hour before he could get up the nerve to go inside.

Whatever he might have expected was nothing like what he found. Men and women were sitting on chairs, rustling sheets of paper and frowning at them. Most people were quiet, almost as if they were in church.

The man nearest to him was sitting on the second step of a ladder and marking sheets furiously before

16

he looked up. "If you have to rubberneck, son, do it in the next county. Please."

Sebastian could hear his heart hammering as he said, "I—I want to be an actor."

There was a murmur of laughter in the room. The man to whom he'd been talking raised a hand for silence from the actors. He wasn't a tall man, but he did have fierce eyes and a nose that twitched like a rabbit's.

"My name is Goldenberg, and I'm the director of this tattered little group," he said. "Money is a consideration here, so that when we need somebody to play the part of a Negro we simply put one of our actors into blackface."

Sebastian found himself twitching miserably at the white man's care and courtesy.

"If I can't be an actor here, where could I be one?"

"At a colored minstrel show, I think."

"Would you call that acting?"

"Of course. Even if you don't feel like working, even if you've just heard terrible news, you have to go up on stage and tell jokes. If that isn't acting, I don't know what is."

"I want to be an actor who says serious speeches."

"Well, I can't put you on the stage right away." Mr. Goldenberg's brows did a little dance. "You have to learn how to do it."

"How do I learn it? Where can I go?"

"There's no single answer," Mr. Goldenberg said finally. "Get an education first, as best you can. Get good books out of the public library and read them. If you don't know what a certain word means, look it up in the dictionary."

"And that's how I'd become an actor?"

"It's a necessary first step, whether or not you become a dark Richard Mansfield," Mr. Goldenberg said. "Get a job where you see many people. Make notes about how they look and walk and talk. Try to figure out how their clothes and posture help to show what they're really like. Learn and observe and remember. Try two years of that, son, and then come back to me and I'll find out if you've learned anything much."

"Two years?" Sebastian's stomach felt hollow.

"If it's any consolation, I promise that you'll get a careful and thorough and impartial hearing. And if you don't know what any of those words mean, you can start your real education by looking them up."

Sebastian thanked Mr. Goldenberg and left. He disappointed his mother by telling her what he wanted.

"Sweet Jesus," Sarah said. "My son is trying to climb into the white man's world!"

He went to work, getting a dock job to watch people and even make drawings of them. He did as much reading as he could, often late into the night, and went to work on as little as five hours of sleep in a night.

His industry may have impressed her, but the acting he sometimes did in front of a mirror used to make her shake her head. She went to church one afternoon and came back after a long talk with the preacher. She laid down the law.

"If you can't make acting money in six months," she said sternly, "you go to see Bedrock Bartholomew instead and let him learn you to be an undertaker. At least you'll never starve none."

Sebastian knew that it would take more than six months to turn into an actor, but he figured he'd go back to those actors in six months and try his best to get a job with them this time.

He was surprised to see so many new faces at the Civic Center rehearsal, including a little blond girl. When he asked for the director, it wasn't the compassionate Mr. Goldenberg who came over to talk to him, but a mustached man who seemed in a hurry.

18

His name was Borradaile and he said briskly that Mr. Goldenberg had been dead for two months.

"What do you want?" he snapped.

Sebastian couldn't make himself sound confident, but was only able to stammer out what he had been doing and that he hoped for a job.

Mr. Borradaile started to shake his head. The little girl in the place, who couldn't have been more than seven years old, piped up:

"I can't work with a nigger because my daddy says that they smell bad."

The director suddenly seemed more interested in annoying the little girl than in helping Sebastian. He asked, "Can you read? I mean, can you perform the physical act of reading?"

"Y-yes, sure."

Half a dozen sheets of paper were handed to him. "Then go to work and read this. For purposes of our audition, you've got the part of Joe. Betsy, you'll do your part as you memorized it."

The little girl who had been spoken to sniffed. "I'll be at the other end of the room."

"He has to stay closer to you than that," the director said maliciously. He told Sebastian, "Get to within six feet of her. That's important for the part."

Sebastian did. The little girl sniffed and then turned the other way. The director said, "You're to start, Betsy."

She turned around, her back to Sebastian, before reciting. Her voice was expressive and she used it well. Sebastian started to speak when it was time for his first words as written on the paper, but the child kept on talking. She was saying every speech of hers as written down, but saying all the words without stopping except for breath. Some of the actors looked as if what was happening could be called funny.

The director finally said, "Betsy, if you don't want me to spank you, then you'll do the scene my way."

The little girl screamed and ran out, closing the door behind her and sobbing bitterly from the other side.

"She'll be back," the director predicted. "Betsy is the sole support of her family, so she'll hear the call of Thespis once again or her dear old daddy will spank her little ass for her."

Sebastian looked at his encouraging smile and said stiffly, "You're hiring me as a scarecrow to keep the brat in order."

"A beginning actor takes his jobs for the reason that they're being offered," the director pointed out.

Sebastian said carefully, "If I can get some lines, I suppose I'll go along with it."

"Not too many lines just yet, but we'll work something out." The director beamed. "Won't our dear little Betsy be delighted!"

The next few weeks were so exciting that Sebastian didn't even pay much attention to Sarah's hard breathing and other signs of returning heart trouble. Tension in his life wasn't caused so much by the little girl who avoided the newcomer whenever she could and kept from talking to him. It was the lines he was given that caused him irritation and even hurt.

"Do you expect me to say, 'I'se gwine 'a he'p you, Missy, for whut ah kin'?"

"That's the line," Borradaile snapped. "You're supposed to be a slave, not an Oxford graduate. I want you to say the line slowly, like it was syrup coming out of a jug. I want you to drawl."

Sebastian gritted his teeth, then tried it.

Borradaile said, "Do it again, lad. Remember that this scene is set in a watermelon patch and the little mistress has come to ask you loyal slaves for help. The other two slaves in this scene will be Sanders and Passy in blackface—Passy used to work in a minstrel show and he looks as black as you do when he puts the stuff on. By the way, do you know any

20

good hymn with the words 'Jesus' and 'promised land' in 'em?"

"I—I suppose so." Sebastian decided he would ask Sarah about that as soon as he got home.

"Good. We'll open with the hymn and then go into the scene and when Betsy exits you boys will all go back to the hymn. And I want it to be the most goddamn religious hymn there ever was."

Sebastian was thinking that he wouldn't invite a yellow dog to the theatre to see him, let alone his mother. In fact, he wouldn't tell Sarah exactly what he was doing, but would give her the impression that he was being permitted to watch from backstage.

On the night of the first public performance, Sebastian was so nervous that he stepped outside for a breath of air. Nobody saw him leave. When he started to the stage entrance again he was stopped by the surly looking doorman.

"No niggers allowed back here!"

"I've been allowed back here since the rehearsals started," Sebastian said spiritedly. "I'm in the show."

"You?" The doorman looked contemptuously down at Sebastian's ragged costume. "Get out, or I'll ram you!"

Sebastian knew better than to argue further. He ran around to the front entrance where he had been told that Borradaile would spend most of the evening. The director wasn't in sight. An usher looked at him icily.

"What do you want, boy?"

"I have to get inside. I'm part of the show."

"You can't get in without a ticket, boy. Can you afford to buy one?"

Sebastian sounded gruffly authoritative now. "Don't be a fool, son. Do I sound like a black? Don't you know blackface make-up when you see it?"

The usher stepped aside respectfully, murmuring, "That looks just like the real thing."

Later on, Sebastian realized that those tense moments helped him forget to be nervous that night on stage . . .

Borradaile seemed to have taken a liking to him and he was getting parts in other shows, but all the parts were those of ignorant darkies. Not once did he get to play the part of a black man who could read and write. He was always cast as a bone-ignorant lazy drifter who was a devil with the girls. He was always using black talk like "laws-a-massey" and "gwine". He was beginning to develop an absolutely murderous hatred for that non-word "gwine." It was becoming a symbol of everything that was wrong with the world.

His own developing skills must have made Borradaile give Sebastian some meatier parts. There was one show in which he played a black man who wanted to be a doctor, which would have been a step in the right direction when it came to getting better Negro parts. Unfortunately, Borradaile wanted it played for laughs.

"Keep using the nigger talk, Sebastian," Borradaile instructed. "It's an easy laugh, and in this show we need all the laughs we can get."

Sebastian knew he'd better go along with it.

Sarah died while the troupe was rehearsing that play, the first one he'd have wanted her to see in spite of everything. He took one day off for the funeral and one for the mourning. At nineteen he was alone in the world.

His life changed, as if the world was out to make up to him for what he had lost. His parts got longer and he was making more money. Best of all, probably, his love life started to look up.

He was romancing a girl named Coralie, who he had met a few days after the funeral. Coralie was fine in bed, warm and sweet and willing. She said

22

she had a kid, a daughter, but before the month was out he knew that she'd given birth to five children, each of them by a different man. He said he'd had enough and walked out.

After that he spent a few months with a girl named Bianca, who wasn't nearly so willing in bed but was more respectable.

At a morning rehearsal for a new play, Borradaile gave the company some news. "We've been invited on a summer tour at a time when we wouldn't be working anyhow. It's a four-state tour and it'll help fill our pockets for a change."

The director glanced over at Sebastian, who was applauding with the others. Afterward, he called Sebastian over for a private talk.

"We'll be touring in Georgia, Alabama, Mississippi and South Carolina, I'm afraid," Borradaile said. "Your job will be intact even if you don't want to come along."

"I think I'd like to go," Sebastian said, his decision made before Borradaile had finished. "Aside from the extra money, I want to see what the South is like and just how bad it is for my people. I want to know the part I'm acting when I get cast as a slave in the future."

"I hinted that you might have trouble, lad, and I wasn't funning. You're almost sure to see a number of ugly incidents, maybe even to be part of one or two. The last time I did a tour of the South I saw a lynching. About fifty colored had been lined up to see what happened to some Negro who had worn a white man's hat by accident. That was the reason he died, believe it or not, Sebastian—for wearing a white man's hat!"

"I always hear about these things or read about them, but I ought to see how bad it is." Mr. Goldenberg's advice had never left his mind. "The more experience I get, the better it is for my acting."

"I suppose that's true." Borradaile shrugged.

"Suit yourself, lad, but don't blame me when something goes wrong."

A deep Southern voice belonging to a white man said, "The coon's waking."

Sebastian opened his eyes part way on haze and darkness. He was in Georgia and had been hit on the head by a beggar. Something under him was moving, so he took it for granted he was in a carriage. This whole business must have happened on account of that white fool he'd had to manhandle in order to keep the actors on stage from being disturbed. That white hog must be taking this way to get even with him. For the first time Sebastian felt a flick of fear.

Another white voice said, "Lay on him again, will you? I don't want to have to worry 'bout no coon."

Sebastian knew it was coming but couldn't dodge. There was a moment of great pain and then everything went black and he wasn't able to be afraid. Not for a while, at least.

Chapter Two

Eli Crosby's plans had been simple enough when he started to ride with Grace in his carriage. He would let her off at Rootstock and then he would lead the waiting carriage on to his plantation. He would work over the black man who had offended him at the theatre.

His plans suddenly changed, though, and it was Grace who changed them without knowing it. She had become quiet, calm, unusually thoughtful. Her face was suddenly soft, the eyes large and wistful, the lips gently downturned at the corners. Eli Crosby saw what he thought were the signals given by a woman in the mood for some love and wondered if this would be the night for Grace Parker to give in to him.

He didn't know that she was thinking about the black actor she had seen on stage. He had made an impression on her, showing force of character and a careful knowledge of what he was doing. The whites had some acting ability, heaven knew, but she wasn't used to seeing a black outdo a white. It was as if this realization had suddenly stimulated her jaded imagination and lifted her depressed spirits.

Too, she had been impressed by his good looks. She had felt certain stirrings of the sort that a wellbred white woman is not supposed to feel at the thought of a black.

She wanted to think about that.

Eli Crosby, looking at the face of a woman he desired, rubbed his chunky hands together and hoped he wasn't sweating too much. Every so often a bordello girl would say something about sweat and he'd wave it away and say that he wanted what he had come there to get. But he supposed it wasn't attractive for a nice woman to see.

The carriage halted in front of Rootstock, and he got off and helped Grace down.

"I'd ask you inside," she began absently, "but—"

Crosby sighed loudly. "It seems a shame to have taken an attractive girl to the theatre and not even be asked for a drink afterwards."

"Very well," she said reluctantly and led the way to the house. Crosby had never liked the fragile-looking furniture or walls done in pink. A damned waste of money. When he was master here, things would be done differently. Differently and better—both.

Grace clapped her hands for a house slave who appeared after a time.

"One bourbon, please, for Mr. Crosby."

"I certainly wouldn't drink alone."

"Two, then," she ordered. "And please hurry."

Crosby finished his drink in four gulps, wiped his mouth with his hand, burped, then smiled in embarrassment. Luckily, though, Grace hadn't been listening to him.

She was sitting on a pink-striped couch. A breeze through the louvered windows ruffled her bright blond hair, but she didn't appear to notice that, either. Crosby walked over and sat beside her. His hand rested on her knee.

"Was it a good evening for you, Grace?"

"Up to this point, yes," she said, smiling faintly.

His hand rose. Grace shifted to her right, got up and made a point of fixing some little ornament. When she sat down again, though, it was in one of the chairs.

Crosby stood and advanced to the chair, towering over her. "Grace, dear, let's be together for the night."

"If that's the sort of thing you want," she said mildly, "I would think you could go into town and find yourself some fancy woman there."

"I want you," he said thickly.

28

He sank down on his haunches, hands wandering across her breasts through the dress. He kept his body close to her, wanting her to feel his need. But her face showed no sympathy.

With both hands she gently eased his hands away from her body and moved the light chair back very slightly.

"I'm not going to that sort of thing tonight, Eli. I'm sorry."

"You say 'tonight' as if the two of us were doing it every night," he said bitterly. "What do you want from me? Marriage? I've offered that."

"And I haven't made up my mind about accepting."

"Perhaps we ought to get to know each other better."

"Not tonight, Eli. Not tonight."

He thought her voice had changed slightly when she said those final words. She stood up rather than look at his face or see his distended need. He got up, too, angry but in some control of himself.

They said goodnight in a perfunctory way. Grace went up to her bedroom and changed into soft silk nightwear. Outside she heard Crosby's voice raised for a moment, then stillness. His carriage drove off. Was it her imagination or did a second carriage leave the grounds, too?

Eli Crosby, bumbling outside and walking angrily to his carriage, had been half-stopped by the sound of a whistle. He looked around to see one of the white beggars he had hired earlier. The beggar stood in front of the second carriage Crosby had hired to transport the black man. He was holding a hand out and rubbing the thumb against four fingers in rapid succession. No doubt he wanted money.

"Follow me and you'll get it," Crosby said. "But before you do," he told the ragged white man and his friend, who was looking anxiously out of a window, "tie up the coon at the whipping post," Crosby ordered. "I'll start off fith fifty lashes soon as I'm ready."

Actually, he supposed he'd take a few winks of sleep before doing the work he looked forward to.

The beggar said something then. Crosby's face reddened even more than had become natural. He stared into the carriage, then whirled on both beggars and let out a string of murderous oaths.

Tim, the beggar who had found the job for his friend, had been impatient since this grand carriage swung into the grounds of Rootstock. He felt he didn't belong anywhere near such an expensive place.

"The boss said we take the black to his place and then dump him. This is where we stop."

"Are you sure this is his place?" his friend said. John was tall and thin, with a straggly mustache. "Where'd the boss drive to?"

Tim caught hold of Sebastian by the armpits, palms upwards, and waited. He had to lead the way out. Ten feet from the carriage, in humid night air, he stopped and cursed.

"Stop playing games and help me take him to the overseer," Tim said finally. "He'll know where the whipping post is . . . all right, damn it, stay here with him and I'll bring the overseer."

He glanced back once to see that the carriage driver, himself colored, was looking ahead of him into the night as if nothing had happened among the two white beggars and their black captive.

Tim walked slowly and carefully along unfamiliar ground. There was a quartet of wooden cabins at the far end of a plain. He supposed the overseer lived in one of the painted ones.

30

He was halfway to the place when a rough voice growled, "State your business on these grounds. I'm Ryder, the overseer."

Tim whirled. He was looking at a white man with dark hair mostly covered by a floppy straw hat. He wore white pants and a shirt. In one hand he carried a dog whip.

"I've got a darkie for you," Tim said.

"Selling, I s'pose." The overseer didn't see Tim's grin at the notion of selling the black man to this overseer. "Where is he?"

Ryder followed the beggar, smiling at the notion of buying the slave for a few dollars and charging Miss Grace two times as much. His mind was working overtime.

The beggar stopped. Ryder bent over and touched the black man's calves, then prodded his arms.

"Hasn't done much work, I'd say."

"You can make him stronger," Tim bargained. "If we do good business here, I'll bring you the others I get."

"He's not worth a penny more than twenty-five dollars," the overseer said. "Carry him to the slave quarters."

"I'll take the money first."

"In that case, I'll carry him myself." Ryder put the dog whip between his belt and pants, then stooped over and lifted Sebastian by the armpits. "You come back for the money tomorrow. I don't have a penny with me."

Tim cursed inwardly. The Rootstock overseer would later deny ever having seen him. Well, at least he had done the job that the boss would be paying for.

At the second place, the boss again told them to string up Sebastian on the whipping post, and Tim looked blank.

31

"But we left him over there. At the other place. At Rootstock."

The boss let out a string of oaths and told the coachman to drop the bunglers, as he called them, a mile before the town of Tremont. They'd have to do some walking before the night was over. He threw several coins after them as the carriage was getting under way.

"We always get the short end," John said sadly.

It was Tim who saw the bright side. "It isn't every day, though, that we get a chance to work for a gentleman."

Sebastian must have slipped into a normal sleep during the night. He was waked up by the sound of a horn blowing.

For a moment he was perfectly still. On all sides he heard people moving, groaning, yawning and making any number of wake-up noises. He lay on straw that moved when he did. A bug stepped on his body, and he killed it with a hand-slap against a naked thigh. He had never smelled anything like the odor out here in all his life.

Shabby-looking colored men moved in the hut. Sebastian croaked out a few words and one man turned to talk back to him. Sebastian blinked, startled.

"I don't understand your accent," he said slowly.

Another man, talking loudly, said, "You lay there, boy, and a whip comes at you soon."

Sebastian understood only two or three words, but tried to keep from realizing where he was.

"This is a mistake," he said loudly and clearly as he could. "I'm free. I don't belong here. I'm free."

"Not now," a slave said tauntingly. "Get used to it, boy, 'cause that's how it is or you get slapped around for not being obedient, not knowing your place."

Sebastian shook his head forcefully, beginning to

32

follow the musical and lazy-sounding speech. He had tried to talk like it in a show once, and missed by a mile.

He got to his hands and knees, then realized that he was naked. One of the slaves was putting on the pants that Sebastian had worn, and finally tossed him a dirty pair. The others laughed. The man who had taken his shirt tossed him one that looked as if moths had dined on it. He wasn't given underclothes.

"What about shoes?" he asked tiredly. "Whoever's got my shoes could at least give me his old ones."

An older man, arms akimbo, paused in the doorway. "You find yourself with a pair of shoes out here, boy, and you get whipped for a biggety nigger who don't know his place."

Another slave asked, "You want a pair of shoes of your own, boy?" He rubbed his stomach. "You won't get none."

The sour smell came to Sebastian's nostrils again, and he looked at the slaves laughing as they got out of the barn or hut or whatever it was. They behaved as if they had never heard anything so funny in their lives.

It surprised Sebastian that people of his own race should do such things to him and that others of his race thought it was a clever thing to have done. He wondered why he didn't feel pity for people who had been slaves all their lives, but decided that they were like cruel children, all of them, and he didn't really care what might happen to any of them as long as he could get away from here. It shocked him to feel so strongly about that, and he didn't like himself a hell of a lot because he did feel that way.

He half-crawled to the door. A number of slaves were eating listlessly, without knives or forks or spoons. It wasn't daylight yet, and his feet were scalded from such close contact with bare boards and earth, but he was glad to get out of that stinking cabin.

"There he is, our visitor," the mean-looking slave said mockingly at sight of him. This was a fellow with a hooked nose, thick lips and a jutting jaw. There wasn't a hair on his head. He looked powerful as well as mean.

Strung up to the edge of his endurance, Sebastian gritted his teeth and snapped, "Shut your miserable mouth."

The mean-looking slave started to get up. Sebastian was looking forward to a fight, a chance to release the tension that had become part of him, that lived in him now.

Just as he started to make his charge, a whistle sounded shrilly. A white man had walked into the area, having gone through the house and out the door. He was dressed in white, with a straw hat that hid most of his dark hair. In his right hand he carried a dog whip.

"I don't want none of you boys fooling around, including you, Rufus."

The mean-looking slave's face looked as if it had been stained by red. The overseer turned to Sebastian.

"As for you, I bought you last night and if you don't behave I send you back in pieces. And don't think I wouldn't do it, property or not."

Sebastian said nothing, but that wasn't satisfactory to this white man, either.

"I'm Jack Ryder, Mister Jack to you, and don't you forget the mister," the overseer said. Lightly, then, he punched Sebastian in the forearm. "But if you're obedient, boy, and you can be trusted, I might use you like a personal helper of mine. We'll see."

First the stick and then the carrot. No doubt the overseer could find a hundred ways to put off giving any slave an easier job.

34

He turned to the others. "Was breakfast okay, boys? Good. Now we get a day's work out of of you. Hop into the wagons and move along. On the double, now."

Fifty slaves walked to the four wagons with their tired-looking horses. Sebastian actually looked forward to it. The fields would be wide, and there'd be plenty of room for him to get away. He'd be back in Tremont with the other actors long before sundown.

The wagons were stopped in the middle of a large field, and the sullen slaves, eyes closed, were joined by two wagons with women in them. If they hadn't been in the way of his probably escape route, through a line of trees, he'd hardly have noticed them. They wore handkerchieves on their heads. Their dresses were tattered. Few of them were young and the young women weren't especially pretty. Some of the men called out.

An alert young one, smiling at Sebastian, had to glance at Rufus when the mean-looking slave walked towards her. But she said, "He's the bastard of the place, Rufus is."

Rufus growled. "You watch your tongue, gal."

But the gal was talking to Sebastian. "Every plantation needs one complete bastard. It kind of makes things balance out. Over here, it's Rufus. A very important boy, Rufus is."

She grinned at Sebastian. For the first time he saw her as a cheerful little thing with surprisingly merry eyes and a pert little snub nose. To his own surprise, he smiled at her.

She said, "Let's see each other later on."

He smiled. "Yes, let's do that."

She looked startled. "You sure talk funny. It's like you had a shovel in your mouth."

He couldn't have imagined a more difficult time for him to run into a person he felt sure he could like.

"What's your name?" he asked as the other girls started to move away. "Tell me your name."

But she chuckled, moving with the others, and glanced back at him. "Can't figure out a word you say, not a single word."

She was laughing gently as she walked away from him. Sebastian was going to ask the nearest slave for what he wanted to know, but there was no reason in the world for him to find out. He'd be getting away from here in a short time.

It was Rufus who gave him the information without any idea of how important it would become.

"What a gal, that Orchid," he said to them all. "She can cheer up anybody and she means it."

The last wagon stopped, letting the overseer out. He approached the men, dog whip in his right hand.

"I want a detail to widen the road," he said, looking directly at Rufus. "We're having too much trouble getting the wagons out. It'll need five boys."

The hairless slave picked four who seemed strong. With a mocking smile he gestured at Sebastian.

"He's stronger than he looks, *buckra*," Rufus said to the frowning overseer. "I'm the best driver we've got, and I know."

Sebastian joined the others on the way to the last wagon. Picks and shovels had been hauled out, and one tool was given to each man. Sebastian, carrying a pick, started walking to a grassless pathway.

"We can start here and dig up to there," Rufus said. "Be enough work in the morning after I get finished up with the little weasel over here."

Rufus made and unmade fists. The other men made a half-circle around him. Sebastian raised the pick menacingly, but two men grabbed his arm and forced the pick out of it. With that done, they kept hands on him.

"Get his pants down," Rufus ordered. "We'll give him a real good time."

Sebastian tried to kick the slave who came close

36

to him,.but that slave punched him in the stomach and he doubled up. By the time he could straighten out, he realized his pants had been taken off.

"Big as a horse and smooth as a baby," Rufus said. His voice sharpened. "Now get him back of the trees and out of sight. Push him from behind! Use the knee! That's right."

Pressure under his sex kept him from stopping. He called out.

"Cover him on the mouth," Rufus said, and a hard black hand covered his mouth painfully. He was tied to a tree, face toward it.

"You put your legs apart when you get told," Rufus warned, seeing the legs tight together, "or you get reamed where it hurts like hell."

Sebastian's pants were down around his feet. Apart from the terror and the total indignity, he was chilly as well. It was the suddenness with which this was happening that was so profoundly depressing; the lack of any advance warning. His life had been set and steady until he had come to the South, and now any wind of sudden violence might carry him away.

"I'm first," Rufus said irritably, right behind him. "Spread the legs apart, boy, or God help you."

From the clearing, just beyond the trees, Sebastian heard the overseer's gruff voice.

"Where are they?" Ryder was asking gruffly. "Somebody yelled just a minute ago and I want to know who and why."

Sebastian turned in time to see Rufus gesture to the other boys. One of them started to pick up his pants and the others began working swiftly at the ropes.

Rufus whispered to Sebastian, "One word 'bout this to anybody at all and you turn into a dead man."

The others worked swiftly as heavy footsteps came closer, but they weren't quick enough. The overseer plunged through the outer covering of trees in time to see Sebastian still tied and the pants around his midriff but far from being buttoned.

"What's all this?" the overseer demanded.

Rufus sounded mildly upset. "Jus' trying to teach this boy a lesson, Mister Jack."

"That isn't what it looks like."

"He's lazy. Said he had to do something, you know, to move his insides. A lot of time went past, but he didn't come back. I went after him and there he was with his pants down, but he was faking. So I had him tied here. He put up a holler, but it won't do him no good."

The overseer asked Sebastian, "Is that true, boy? What have you got to say for yourself?"

A hand had been removed from Sebastian's mouth, but he could still feel its presence as he tried to clear his throat. The overseer had become impatient by the time Sebastian said quietly:

"I've been told I'll get killed if I tell you the truth of what happened."

The overseer hadn't heard. In his impatience he had turned to Rufus. "I suppose you want him to get five of the best."

"Yes, Mister Jack."

"All right." But the overseer didn't move into position where he could use the dog whip across Sebastian. "You're the driver for these men today, Rufus, and you've got the right to hit with five. Use this dog whip of mine."

Sebastian had tried to move his body so he could turn to face the overseer as best he could and talk directly to him. It was too late to stop the whipping, but not a completely useless motion for him to have made.

"Across the back," the overseer warned, having been briefly caught by the sight of Sebastian's nakedness. "No whacks on the ass."

It meant the saving of some small dignity, at least.

38

The first crack of the dog whip thundered across his back, its impact nearly pulverizing him. The pain was sheer agony. He called out, even though he had told himself he wouldn't make a sound. At the second descent of the whip he was keeping his lips shut tightly. The pain wasn't such a fierce shock and he was able to control himself, but some noise did escape through his jaw.

Two more times the dog whip lanced across Sebastian's back.

"And now," Rufus gritted, "for the best one of all."

The leather thong, half an inch wide, made a snake-hiss in the air. Nothing else happened. The whip hadn't come down for the fifth time.

Sebastian tried to look around but could see nothing. He was only able to turn his head part of the way to take note of the others. He did see the elongated shadow of a horse when he stretched his neck, though, and took it for granted that there had been an interruption.

A white woman's voice said, "What's going on here?"

Sebastian supposed that the woman had been riding over this plantation and that she carried considerable authority. The horse pawed the ground restlessly.

"Mr. Ryder, didn't I tell you that I wanted no whipping on this plantation? Are you incapable of listening? I want that boy set free of those ropes."

When the ropes were cut off, the rush of blood back to his body brought him nearly as much pain as the last whip-crack would have done. Sebastian had to grit his teeth to keep from calling out with fresh pain. He turned slowly again.

He was looking at an attractive, blond white woman astride a horse. She had moved forward. She wore riding clothes. Her eyes were cornflower-blue, her skin clear, her chin trembling lightly.

Sebastian found himself not able to say what he wanted to. He wanted to say that he was a free man and that he would prove it to her if he had a chance. Here was his one opportunity to talk to somebody with great power and he was too shaken-up by the whipping to try, let alone to be convincing. His tongue was planted to the roof of his mouth, it seemed, and his hands were warm and sweaty.

His pants had been buttoned for him, he saw gratefully, but he still felt naked in front of the blond. She saw it, but made no comment. It was when she suddenly looked at his face that her mouth grew slack and her eyes widened.

"But you're the one who—" she started, and Sebastian knew that in spite of being in this place in these clothes, he had been recognized.

"Yes, Miss," he said, careful to make his voice deeper and more theatrical than usual. He found the courage to go on. "You must have been at the theatre last night."

She nodded, then said, "Go to the main house and wait for me."

Ryder, still surprised, turned to one of the others. "Sam, go with him."

The new boy said rigidly, "Walk behind me, Sam, not with me."

Grace Parker turned her horse around and left for the clearing, probably to go back to the stables.

Ryder, wanting to show his authority, whirled on Rufus. "Finish the job with three men and you'd better do it well." He raised the dog whip briefly, then turned away from the dismayed blacks.

Chapter Three

Sebastian looked longingly over toward the road, but decided against suggesting to Sam that the two of them make an escape. Sam looked angry and seemed to be having a hard time controlling himself.

A house slave took one look at Sebastian and snapped that he wouldn't be admitted unless Miss Grace did it personally. The sun had become warm, and Sebastian wondered how slaves could work from sunup to sundown in this hellish weather.

Grace Parker, in a white dress and with lace ruffles at the throat and sleeves, found Sebastian waiting in front of the main house. She smiled lightly, walked inside, and in a moment the house slave appeared with a pair of slippers, which he put down on the porch. He left without having looked at Sebastian.

"Put these on so you won't get the floor dirty," Grace Parker said. "I needed to do some bargaining with Alfred before he'd let you come in."

His eyes were on the blond's figure as she walked into the sunny parlor, furnished in a brightly feminine style. She suddenly turned, catching his eyes on her, and gave a slight smile.

"My name is Grace Parker. I own this plantation, Rootstock," she said, sitting in front of a portrait of a mustached Army man with a cutlass in one hand. "It doesn't matter how you got here, really, and I suppose you know that Southerners are hot-blooded people, never far from violence or passion."

"My back knows that," he said.

"If you had received twenty lashes it very well might know it better," Grace Parker observed.

Sebastian asked bluntly, "When can I go?"

"As soon as you've heard me out," she said softly and raised a well-tended hand. "I don't doubt you're thinking whether to use violence against me. If you control yourself I'll show you why you'd be

43

foolish to do it. By the way, your name is . . . Sebastian? It's very rare for a colored person in this area not to have a fancy name. Very rare indeed."

He waited.

"You've probably heard, Sebastian," she said carefully, "that white men have gone to bed with colored gals who worked for them as slaves. The gals keep on working and nothing more is said. The white master has satisfied his lust and there's an end to it."

"I've heard of that sort of thing," Sebastian admitted.

"Let's suppose now that the white person involved is a woman," Grace Parker said. "She is attracted to a slave and can do nothing about getting him between the sheets. If the man is not a good slave he'll brag for a long time. If he is sold to another, he will continue the bragging. The woman will get a bad reputation, which is one of the things she doesn't want."

"I suppose that's true," Sebastian said, puzzled by what he was hearing and not able to understand why she had gotten him into this conversation at all.

"But let's think of the problem in another way, Sebastian. Let's suppose that the woman wants to be with a colored boy who won't talk afterward because he is really free and he belongs in the North. Furthermore, he has no friends among the coloreds at the plantation and will leave as soon as the affair is finished."

She was looking directly at him. Sebastian nearly drew back and wanted to hide his face with both hands.

"You—you mean this?"

"I told you that Southern people are sudden in their responses," Grace Parker said thoughtfully. "It goes with the climate, I believe."

He couldn't bring himself to look at her, let alone say a word.

44

"I think you'll have to work during the day, but I can tell Jack Ryder not to give you any difficult chores. At night, you come to the main house by the back way. Do you see any objections to that?"

"It can't work," Sebastian said instantly, then tried to figure out a reason. "The overseer will know something's wrong if you tell him not to let me do hard jobs. So you see the whole idea can't pay off."

"No, wait! I'll make you a house slave and perhaps we can even take odd moments during the day. I wouldn't want you to be too tired, you know."

Sebastian was on the point of saying that he had never in life heard anything stranger.

"It won't work," he said automatically, but couldn't figure out any reason to back up what he was saying.

"Why not?" she taunted him. She broke the silence that followed. "It'll work so well that I'm sure you can't disagree."

"And what if I say no? What if I don't want to do it?"

"Why, that'll make things all the more interesting, Sebastian, until you change your mind and start to enjoy what's natural. You certainly aren't unnatural."

It crossed his mind to try and act as if he did happen to be strange.

"And if you say you are, Sebastian, I'll call in one slave who I know really is queer and I'll see how two men do that sort of thing. It might be very interesting."

Remembering what had come so close to happening at the tree not long ago, Sebastian closed his eyes and shuddered.

"Suppose I won't do anything at all of that type or any other type?"

She shrugged. "In that case, Sebastian, I don't have any reason to care what happens to you one way or the other. I don't care if you stay in the fields till you can't work there any longer because of old age."

"You'd let that happen?"

"I wouldn't stop it. I simply wouldn't care."

He would have to agree to what she wanted, of course, but he knew he needed to get the best possible terms for himself.

"I can't stay here forever."

"The longer you stay, the greater my danger." Grace Parker considered it. "I'll make you a promise I can keep, Sebastian. In one month you'll be free. One month only. One month for a light fling, and less if I find myself dissatisfied." Her eyes roamed his body. "I don't think that will happen, though. Well, Sebastian?"

If he was a house slave for the next month, he'd have more energy to escape. He'd try not to let himself become a slave to this woman, a slave by day and by night as well.

"If any white person found out about it, I could get myself hanged."

"No white person will find out and no dark person, either," she promised.

There was a light knock on the parlor door and it opened on the house slave, Alfred, who looked as if he had just swallowed a prune with the pits and all.

"Mister Eli Crosby is here to see you, Miss."

"Let him wait a moment, Alf . . ."

The door opened further on the chunky white man.

"I didn't want to wait," he started, then he smiled grimly. "This is the man I came to see you about, Grace. I own him and there's plenty of unfinished business between us."

He rubbed his hands together. It had been a difficult day for him, what with supervising so many people and thinking only about his trip to Rootstock to pick up one slave. He must have taken three drinks already.

46

"This is one of my house slaves," Grace said softly. "Say that he isn't, Eli, and you'll have lost me forever as a friend." In a different voice she said, "You may leave now, Sebastian."

Sebastian turned to go, the welts on his back hurting in spite of the thin shirt as he moved. Back of him he heard Eli Crosby burst out laughing. Sebastian couldn't help turning slightly if only to look at the man nearly doubled up with obscene mirth. Eli Crosby finally straightened, then wiped eyes and lips. His hands shook slightly as he put the cambric handkerchief back into a display pocket.

"I can see the welts on his back in spite of that shirt," Eli Crosby finally said. "You're having him treated right, over here. Maybe you're doing it yourself. On my word, Grace, you've got more spirit than I thought you did. I don't feel too bad about leaving him here. Not any more."

When Sebastian left, Eli Crosby was still trying to control his laugher.

The slave called Sam was still waiting, so Sebastian walked straight ahead.

A number of strong-looking boys were lazing around the slave quarters, so he swerved in the direction of the slave cemetery where he might take a few minutes to himself. He nearly bumped into the pert and cheerful little slave girl called Orchid. She was walking slowly, head forward. At sight of Sebastian she straightened and smiled.

"Hello again," he said, feeling a pang. "How come no slaves are working at midday?"

"It's too hot," Orchid said and laughed. "It's hard to figure what you're saying, boy. You talk funny."

"I'm funny, all right." He wasn't sure what made him do it, but he did a few steps of a circus clown imitation that had been a big success in some show. "Don't you know what a circus clown is?"

She was smiling cheerfully, but she shook her

47

head. "I dunno what's a circus or what's a clown. I'm just a slave gal, boy. My old lady worked for Miss Grace's daddy, and I don't know anything 'bout my own daddy except I know what he was. That much I do know, all right."

"What was he?"

"A stud, that's what. A slave for one of the breeding plantations. Miss Grace's daddy would take some of the nigger gals to that place once in a while so they could get young 'uns from the studs."

Sebastian forced a gentle smile to his lips, and felt sorry he wouldn't see her after his escape. How she had managed to stay such a sweet and good person in spite of her circumstances was something Sebastian didn't think he would ever understand.

"Are there any stud farms these days?"

"Sure, but Miss Grace doesn't use 'em for us. She just lets it happen between her gals and her boys."

"Have you had any kids?"

"No, and I wouldn't unless I could keep the man with me, too. A kid without no father isn't likely to grow up good. A baby needs two parents to love it as much as you can love a child."

He asked softly, "Orchid, would you get away from this place if you could?"

"Get out of Rootstock?" Her voice was soft, too, but she sounded puzzled. "Where could I go? What could I do?"

"You could go up North with me," Sebastian insisted. "You'd be all right."

"Up North isn't like paradise, boy," she said. "I hear the whites got all the money and they don't know you're alive. Your own people are just as bad 'cause they try and eat you up when they can."

"It's a different sort of life, sure, but you have to pay for being free."

"I don't think as I'd be able to do it. I don't know how. If I'd got started before, it might not be so bad. But it's too late now."

48

"Is it, Orchid?" he asked carefully. "Even if I'm there, would it still be too late?"

He wanted the answer more than anything else in the world just then, but all that Orchid did was to look from left to right and then back to him.

"Too many ears all around," she decided. "Let's go where we can talk."

She led him past a grove of trees and over to the slave cemetery. There wasn't a headstone to be seen, only sticks in the shape of a cross. No name had been written on any plot.

"I come here when I want to think, but a lot of folks use it for love making." She sat down at one side and gestured him to join her.

"The last boy who tried to get away got beat to death by Mister Jack," she said, answering his question carefully. "He's laying right over there."

"Has a gal ever tried getting away?"

"Don't think so, but her life wouldn't be worth a cotton boll when she got brought back."

"She might make it out of here," he pointed out. "Is your life worth much right now? You're at the beck and call of people who despise you and who you certainly hate in return. If you don't hate these whites, you're not human."

She reached out a hand to touch him, but looked away. "You're a tempter," she whispered. "A tempter."

"We can get away at night," he said eagerly, leaning forward. "I'm not alone up North. I can make money for us and see that we live pretty well."

"Be close to me when I wake up," Orchid said quietly.

Sebastian blinked. He had heard that Southerners lived at the top of their feelings, good or bad, and had seen it. He was becoming the same way himself.

"I can't—can't do this thing," Orchid said, and some of the life went out of her eyes. "My feeling for you is good, but if you try to get away you'll die.

49

Stay here with me. We can have kids. When we get too old to work, I can guard the kids of the younger slave gals while they go out to the field, and you can work in the garden or with the leaves or what all needs to be done that an older boy can do. Like Pappy Jonas, for instance."

"I don't want that," Sebastian said fiercely. "I'm going to be free and if you don't want to join me . . ."

"You're going to be here or half-dead."

He sat down beside her. Without having any idea how it happened, she was in his arms and they were lying back on the hot grass.

"I don't want to do this so soon," Orchid whispered. "I'm not one of those silly loose gals."

"It's now or no other time," Sebastian whispered back fiercely. "I'm getting out of here and you won't go. That means there'll never be another chance for us."

"But not soon, not so soon."

"Now or not at all."

"Not so soon, not so—"

He covered her lips with his, and his hands roamed her body. Breasts not too large or small, midriff without a spare inch of flesh, thighs that had little extra meat on them, legs firmly shaped. Their clothes were off and he examined the wonder that was Orchid's body . . . the nipples that were shaped so beautifully, with little upraised points of reddened flesh around them. She kissed him hard, and then her hands signalled him to get on top of her. He did, blood roaring in his ears. In a few moments it was over and they lay looking and smiling and touching each other.

"Now won't you stay?" she sighed. "I could love you forever, Sebastian, but that don't mean you're not a damn fool."

50

Chapter Four

Sebastian didn't see Grace Parker during what was left of that day, but he didn't have any chance to escape, either. An emergency had come up with the vegetable crop and every male slave pitched in to work hard. The crop was supposed to be their winter food so they didn't hold off. Every one of them had heard about what had happened over at the Hammer place a few years ago when the crops went bad and Mr. Hammer put his slaves on short supplies instead of buying from anybody else.

He was as tired as the others when he went to sleep on the straw pallet. The sudden lowing of a cow woke him, but it woke some others, too. He had to wait until they were back to sleep.

Quietly, he got up and moved to the door. If anybody tried to stop him he'd say he was going to relieve himself, and say it in the dirtiest words he knew. The outer door wouldn't open, though, until his clawing fingers lifted the metal bar across it.

He moved swiftly through the moonless night, having decided to go to the right. The crunch of gravel underfoot may have been too loud, but he knew he was on a road.

A solid barrier of flesh stopped him and he fell back shakily. A bull's-eye lantern shone in his face before he could move.

"What are you doing out here, boy? This is Mister Jack."

Sebastian drew both hands over his eyes, rather than be blinded. "I'm not up to anything. I was on my way to—to the main house."

"By the road?" The overseer grunted. "And what were you going to do in the main house, boy?"

"Miss Grace said she wanted to see me."

"Are you looking for trouble, boy? If I don't use the pistol in my hand, I'll whup you at the post."

Sebastian held his ground and said carefully, "Miss Grace didn't like it when you let Rufus work on me this morning."

Jack Ryder lowered the lantern, and Sebastian drew both hands away from his eyes.

"Come with me to the main house," the overseer said roughly. "We'll get this straightened out once and for all."

Sebastian had to walk in front of the overseer, moving carefully except when he smacked into a tree. Jack Ryder laughed with sour amusement and raised the lantern.

The outline of the main house came into sight, dirty white in the darkness and much too bright in the places that the lantern light briefly seared.

"No light in any windows," Jack Ryder growled in satisfaction. "That proves you're a liar, boy."

As if he had been heard inside, a light suddenly came on. Ryder let out an oath. The door was opened by the house slave, Alfred.

"Miss Parker's asleep, isn't she?"

"No, Mister Jack, she's at the back of the house. Please stay here and I'll ask if she wants to see you now. If you come in, I'll have to wax the floor all over again."

He closed the door gently in the overseer's face.

Grace Parker appeared in the door, looking comfortable, but tired.

"I was on my night's inspection," the overseer began, "when I saw this boy saying he was on his way to the main house at your request."

"Sebastian, isn't it?" she peered at him. "Yes, Ryder, I have some business with him." Her face didn't have any expression at all. "Just a minute."

Slippers were brought to him by the tyrannical Alfred. The overseer cursed under his breath, but was leaving as the front door closed behind Sebastian. In the time it took to reach the parlor, follow-

54

ing Grace, Jack Ryder could have been halfway across Rootstock.

"I sent Alfred to bed with a hand-signal," she said, and he realized what was on her mind. "We'll go into one of the other rooms. Follow me again, please."

Her approach was so businesslike that he wondered if she kept a schedule: this time for sex? She hardly looked at him as she reached for a lantern and turned to the door. She moved attractively, and if he was only going to spend one night with her he would try to let that night become a hard one for either of them to forget.

"This way," she said.

The lantern gave a blue glow through tinted glass frames that looked like three rows of spectacles. She led him out of the lighted parlor and into a dark room. She sat down softly on the bed, lantern to one side, and gestured at him.

As he waited to figure out what she wanted, she said:

"Take my clothes off."

"I might get 'em dirty."

"In that case you might get me dirty, too." She considered. "Go to the basin in the corner and wash your hands, then come back."

As he was busy washing his hands she murmured, "God knows why I should want to risk my reputation."

Sebastian came back to where she waited. His hands shook as he eased the dress off her body with help, then the petticoats. There was some garment that he didn't know by name, and he took that off more slowly and carefully than if he had not been worried about making a rip in some of the clothes.

"Now you can probably guess another reason why I chose you," Grace said, leaning back on the bed so that he could take off her shoes and stockings.

55

"You've got more delicacy than any of the other boys."

He eased her shoes off and then her stockings. He stripped himself, surprised to look down at his body and see that he wasn't as strong as he had expected. But he did want the woman, so he felt sure there couldn't be any trouble.

"Now you must withdraw as soon as you're going to do the important thing," she warned him. "Otherwise I might find myself with a consequence that I simply won't—no pun intended—bear."

"Yes." He lay down next to her on the bed, the first soft bed he had known in a while. He reached for her breasts, cradling them in his hands. The hands roamed her body and were cupped on her buttocks, which were well-shaped and smooth.

"'Now," she whispered. "Now."

He was on top of her and trying to find the place to put himself into. Breathing jaggedly she gripped his sex and led it to what she knew it wanted. There was a moment of pleasure and then he let out a near moan of dismay.

"I can't do it, I can't!"

A feeling of pain told him the reason: he had spent his energies for a while with the slave girl, with Orchid.

Grace let him out of her and reached for his sex again, rubbing it fiercely almost as if she wanted to tear it off him. It did some good, but not enough.

"That isn't all you've got," she said determinedly. "There has to be more."

He tried to make some response, but then he saw that her head was lower because her body was going down on him. He would have prevented it in order to save himself some pain, but there was no time. She made a fist with her hand around part of his sex, all of it except the tip. Then she caressed the tip with her tongue, making cooing noises at the same time.

56

"Do something for me, then," she cried softly, rising to be face-to-face with him and putting both hands on his shoulders. "You know what I want."

Swiftly, before she could change her mind he drew a finger down to her sex and used it as best he could.

"More, more," she whispered and reached for his hand to add pressure against herself. Her whole body was in motion now, thrusting against him. She began to moan and then make the sort of sounds that he associated with hot water in a warming kettle. He could no longer accept what was happening on the terms she wanted, now that it had become mechanical.

She finally gasped and was quiet. He took his finger out.

"It gets better after the first time with somebody new," she said. "Tomorrow morning I'll put you to work in the house. You can go now."

"Sure," he suddenly grinned, "but I can't get my finger to straighten out. It's gone soft on me."

She laughed, as he had wanted her to. She would be in a good humor, not caring that she was sending him out on the grounds alone. She dressed swiftly and walked to the door with him. Not another word passed between them that night.

Outside, Sebastian turned toward the direction he was convinced led to the main road—and freedom.

"Wrong way," Rufus called out swiftly.

Sebastian saw the dark shape in front of him. "What are you doing out here?"

"Mister Jack sent me to make sure you get back to the pens." Rufus glowered. "He made me say I wouldn't put a hand on you, but get smart with me and I will."

Sebastian was nervous and wary when he got up next morning, having spent time on the straw pallet with his eyes closed rather than sleeping. He managed to avoid Rufus during breakfast. He didn't trust the hairless slave one bit.

After breakfast and a nod from Alfred, who slept in the pens along with the others, the two slaves walked together toward the main house. Alfred, who wore square spectacles, was a lightly-moving man with lips turned down at the corners. He didn't say a word to Sebastian, who was pleased at the silence.

Alfred led him to the stable where. despite the horse smell, he took a shower in the stall that had been set aside for that purpose. Then Alfred went to a closet and changed into the uniform of a house servant. Instead of shoes he wore slippers. Sebastian's eyes bulged at sight of them.

"I leave those at the side of the house when I come to work and take 'em back with me to the stable when I go out for the day," Alfred said softly, his first words to Sebastian.

"Will I need a suit, too?"

"Of course." The older slave frowned. "Wait here and I'll bring a suit."

He was back before any escape of Sebastian's could have taken him far. He carried a suit wrapped in paper across one arm and a pair of slippers in his free hand.

"Shoes and stockings and a towel for the feet are at the side of the house," Alfred said. "Now take a shower and get dressed."

"Thank you. Sebastian is my name, by the way."

"Oh? Not from the South, are you? Not born and raised around here from the way you talk."

"I'm from up North."

"Is it true that there's no slavery up North?"

Sebastian nodded.

"Think of being free." The dandified house slave opened his eyes after a pause and brushed away tears, then stiffened. "Free men must work a lot harder than we do, though. I'm sure about that much."

58

Sebastian's new suit fit fairly well, but the shirt was too tight. Alfred scowled.

"Leave the bottom buttons open, where the jacket won't show them," the older slave decided. "Now we have to polish silver. Be careful with the stuff."

The house slave chores involved some cleaning, too, Alfred told him. When there were guests, Sebastian would bring food to Alfred, who would serve.

Grace Parker wasn't in the house and had probably gone out to see if the plantation was running smoothly.

Early in the afternoon he was given some time to himself. He changed clothes and walked over to the slave cemetery. There was no sign of Orchid, but he sat down to wait for her. He partly closed his eyes. When he opened them again, he saw Rufus hovering over him. The mean slave had put down a fishing pole and a can of worms.

"So you're the new houseboy," Rufus said carefully. "You black bastard, *I* was promised that job."

"Miss Grace changed her mind."

"You got that job with more'n a finger," the mean slave said, stepping back. "Get up. If you're lucky, I'll fix it so you can still love it up with a woman, but you won't work so good as a house boy."

Rufus advanced on him as Sebastian was getting up. Sebastian suddenly lay back and drew up one leg, putting pressure against the back of Rufus' rigid knee. Rufus let out a curse and lost his balance, falling beyond Sebastian's reach and across scattered small rocks.

As Sebastian got to his feet, an opening could be seen at clearing's end. Orchid was in his sight once again. The perky little slave gal looked worried. Rufus climbed to his feet, seeing her glance at the other slave.

"If you're fond of him," Rufus said, "you're not the only one here. The other one is nobody but—"

59

He saw both their looks, then picked up his fishing pole and worm can and hurried away.

Orchid's saucer eyes were on Sebastian. "That isn't true, is it? It could be only one person if what he says is true."

"Forget that and come away with me. I came back to ask you."

"So you can pick up with another whi—well, you know what I mean—when you get tired of me?"

"Come away, Orchid, while we've got time."

She tried to take a step back as if to look at him differently, but he put both arms around her and pulled her closer to him. The closer she was, the more desirable she became. His hand slithered along the front of her, touching and caressing the lines of her breast. She suddenly gasped and looked into his eyes. She had stopped struggling, and a warm smile lighted her face.

"Is that what you've got in mind right now, boy?" she asked softly. "To run?"

"Damn it, no, but there isn't time for the other thing if we really want to make it out of here."

"Let's us make time for the other thing." Orchid gestured. "Over there, honey, between the trees."

She held both his hands in her grasp. For half an hour he was as happy as he had ever been. No girl had ever responded so well to his lovemaking, it seemed to him, and he had never wanted to make another girl so happy.

When they were leaning back together afterwards, she asked softly, "Is this what they mean by love?"

"I don't know." Sebastian's wits were whirling. "It might be."

"It's different from loving a child or a dog." She asked, "Do you think we might get married, Sebastian?"

"When we get away, sure."

"But I've got a lot of friends out here and there's an old barn back of the pens for churchgoing day.

60

Tomorrow, Sebastian, we get married and I go wherever you want. It'll be all right."

"So I have to stay until tomorrow," he said rigidly.

Chapter Five

Eli Crosby was Grace's dinner guest that night. Between glowering at the poker-faced Sebastian, he managed to get so drunk he fell· from the table. Grace, who was dressed in gray satin to show her fair complexion, gave orders softly.

"Bring him out to the carriage," she said. "Sebastian will help."

The two slaves hauled the muttering drunk out to the carriage, but the thing wouldn't start because something had gone wrong with a wheel. It was too dark to fix until morning, Crosby's coachman insisted.

Grace Parker sighed when Alfred brought the news to her. "Put him up in the guest room for tonight, then."

Sebastian recognized the room when Eli Crosby was brought up there. It was the same room where he and Grace Parker had tried to make love last night. He didn't even think that the sheets had been changed.

When he was finished with the others, he whispered to Alfred, "Tell Miss Grace that you and me have got to leave here together because nobody else can get me back my slave pen clothes. Tell her something else if you want to, but make sure that the two of us get out at the same time."

Alfred glanced curiously at him, but didn't say a word. He joined Sebastian in the kitchen only a few moments later. He was smiling slightly.

"I fixed it for you, Sebastian. Let's go."

The only way for the slaves to get out, of course, was by the rear entrance. Grace Parker stood near the door as they left. Alfred touched his forehead respectfully at sight of her. Sebastian, after a pause, did the same thing. Grace smiled and wished them a good night, but her right hand was pointing downwards when she looked at Sebastian.

"I'll see you very soon," she added, having given him her most direct look.

Sebastian knew what she was saying. She wanted him back at the main house as soon as possible. At the very thought of it, he felt a sudden flick of pain below his mid-section. It would certainly be as bad this time as it had been before.

He and Alfred changed into slave clothes. Alfred hadn't said a word to him until Sebastian wished him good night when they were fifty feet from the slave pens. Only then did he become talkative.

"Is it true what Rufus was saying?"

"What would that be?"

"About your carrying on with—" He tossed his head in the direction of the main house.

"Of course it's not true."

Alfred said carefully, "You know what might happen if she gets annoyed? She might sell the whole bunch of us down the river or get you hanged. Or get us all hanged if she thinks she has to do it to keep a secret out of what's been happening."

"There's no secret to keep."

"You've been up North so you don't know some things. Out here when you're a slave you're property and nothing else. They can do anything with you they want. Absolutely anything."

"And we're helpless to do anything back to them?" Sebastian smiled grimly. "Maybe it's a mistake that we never do anything back. Know what I mean?"

"If you keep talking like this, Sebastian, you *will* get us all hanged."

"If you were younger, I think you'd agree with what I say."

He walked off. Most of the slaves were outside trying to get some air. It took time before Sebastian could turn back without having been noticed and head for the main house again. This time nobody saw him. He could have made his escape with no trouble to speak of.

But he would have been alone, and he didn't want that. To escape without Orchid meant leaving part of himself behind. It wouldn't have been an escape.

He stopped to put on his shoes, then walked in by the rear entrance. There was a light in the parlor, and he walked over to it. The door was closed in part and he knocked.

Grace Parker's voice came from behind him as she spoke.

"Go inside, Sebastian," she said quietly. "And don't raise your voice."

She had probably been upstairs. Now she was standing on the bottom step of the rear staircase. In one hand she held a candle on a dish. The candle flickered as he watched, sending her shadow into a mad dance.

He walked into the parlor, leaving the door ajar. She closed it when she came in after him. Lovely as she looked, he wanted nothing more than to be married to Orchid.

Grace drew a finger to her lips as she came closer. She wasn't being amorous, Sebastian decided, but wanted to talk more quietly and forcefully.

"You know he's in the house, of course, still calling out in his sleep."

"I'll be quiet."

"No, you don't understand. I'm thinking that he might very well hear us if we do anything. A man has got well-developed senses when it comes to something like that."

Sebastian, a good actor, looked disappointed instead of revealing his true feelings.

Grace said carefully, "There'll be another time, I promise. There's always tomorrow."

"Yes," he said soberly, thinking that he and Orchid would be far away by then.

He surprised himself by leaning over and kissing Grace Parker tenderly on the mouth. It was a soft kiss, a warm kiss, a friendly kiss. Then he left.

Orchid was at his side when he walked into the slaves' church, the ramshackle old building behind the slave pens. Over one hundred rickety chairs had been jammed into the building and there were a number of slaves who had to stand up along the rear walls. The room smelled of dust and cotton. Two windows with wooden slots instead of glass let in the unrelenting sun.

Orchid led him to a seat near the end of a row in the middle. "We won't have to get out very far. I know you aren't taking your ease right now."

"Damn right I'm not."

The preacher was a circuit-rider who went to a different slave church every Sunday in his round of six plantations. No slave ever saw Brother Thomas in the middle of the week. He was a tall man with spectacles. At one time his nose had been broken and some slaves said he was a professional fighter when he didn't go around preaching. Others said that he was just a Sunday preacher who'd once had his nose busted.

Brother Thomas was carrying a package as he stepped onto the small stage, which was made up of half a dozen thick wooden planks. Carefully he undid the package to show a Bible, and put it down on the scarred wooden lectern.

Sebastian whispered to Orchid, "Why does he hide the Bible in a package?"

Orchid whispered back to him, "Any white man who sees a nigger carrying a book will think that the nigger is getting above himself. It's better not to have the trouble."

Sebastian frowned in anger at the preacher, but Orchid leaned against him and made the clouds go away. She was dressed a little more neatly than he had ever seen her before and her eyes were warm and shiny.

"When do we ask him to marry us?"

"After the preaching is done."

"Probably takes a long time. He looks like he would."

"Not usually he doesn't."

Brother Thomas waited for quiet and then began to talk. Sebastian, hardly listening at first, found himself rising to a pitch of fury as he listened. Brother Thomas was saying that the black man's highest duty in life was to be obedient to the white man, to be a good slave and hope and wait for his reward when he got to Heaven.

Sebastian would have forced himself to be quiet, but some of the people in this audience were nodding sadly and somebody called out, "Amen, brother!"

Sebastian heard his own voice, theatrically trained and resonant, asking loudly:

"Are you in the pay of the whites or really a white man with black paint on him like in a minstrel show?"

Orchid started to say, "Shhh, honey," but he pulled her arm so quickly toward himself that she called out with pain.

In the frozen silence Sebastian shouted, "Our people are slaves! Is that all you can say?"

Brother Thomas, keeping on with his sermon, said, "When the Israelites were put into bondage by the wicked pharaoh of Egypt, they didn't despair."

"And what about the Zealots, Brother Thomas?" Sebastian asked loudly. "Their people had given mankind the Old Testament, but they didn't believe there was a place in Heaven for them if they'd be good slaves. The Zealots were children of Israel who had been enslaved to the Romans. They staged an

69

uprising and fought against their former masters, fighting for their freedom."

There was a shout of approval along with dozens of murmurs. Orchid was sitting with hands over her face, ashamed.

Brother Thomas said quickly, "All that, what he's sayin', is a made-up story. There is nothing about it here in the Good Book. Anybody is invited to come up here and see for himself. Or herself."

Alfred, sitting quietly until then, turned in his seat and said, "There isn't nobody here who can read."

It was Rufus who asked, "What about these Israelite Zealots? Did they kill a lot of whites?"

"Yes, they killed a lot of the oppressors, but they didn't get their freedom," Sebastian said. Cries of deep sorrow exploded in the hall. "The children of Israel were starved out and many of them died and the fight took a long time. When they saw that there was no hope, they killed each other. The men killed their wives and then other men and the last ones took poison rather than go back into slavery."

Brother Thomas wiped his forehead nervously and said, "Let us sing a hymn: *Faithful Servant of the Lord.*" Two voices were raised at the start of the hymn, but several others joined in because the tune was a good one. It came to a stop at last and Brother Thomas asked if there was any immediate spiritual need to be met in the congregation.

Sebastian stood up and pointed at Orchid. "This girl and me, we want you to marry us."

Warily, the preacher asked, "Do you have the written permission of your owner? I can't do it without that."

"Do it and you won't need written permission."

Brother Thomas wiped his spectacles carefully before putting them on again. "Boy, you probably think I said no because of you carrying on during my sermon about the word of the Lord. If I say no and won't give in to your spiritual needs, I suppose

70

some brothers and sisters will feel the same way. In that case, I will ignore the laws and do the marrying now. Please come up here with me."

Sebastian, closest to the end of the aisle, left it first. Orchid followed, eyes downcast.

It was Rufus who shouted, "You can't marry them two, Brother Thomas."

It was quiet in the hall. Sebastian whirled to see where Rufus was sitting. Orchid, who had kept walking, came up against Sebastian and moaned softly.

"Because that boy is doing something that is a stink in the nose of the Lord," Rufus said. "He's whoring with another woman."

A sob was torn loose from Orchid's throat.

Sebastian said carefully, "It's not true."

His voice could hardly be heard above the murmurs that had broken out. Angrily, he walked up to the stage, Orchid following. He felt no pleasure at standing in front of an audience once more.

Brother Thomas shrugged, "I can't marry you when there's an objection, brother. Can't and won't."

Orchid left the stage and nearly ran out the opened door. Sebastian threw a look of hatred toward Rufus, then followed.

He found Orchid near the cemetery, her head bent over as she sobbed.

"We tried doing it your way and we couldn't," Sebastian said. "Now will you do it like I said?"

"Just—just let me say a few goodbyes."

"There's no time for that any more."

She raised her tear-stained face to his and said determinedly, "There has to be time, Sebastian."

Jack Ryder was sitting down in the comfortable parlor chair. It was Sunday when Miss Grace asked her overseer in for half-an-hour's talk about the way things were going. Ryder didn't mind. Sundays generally got on his nerves anyway, reminding him that he was an unmarried man who worked around stinking slaves all the time. He sat on the chair he liked best, cradling his drink in two hard hands, shaking his head softly.

"Nothing bad is happening in Rootstock at all, Miss Grace," Ryder said, pursing his lips so that they almost looked like wet red flowers. "I certainly don't see no trouble comin'."

"Ah." She sighed. "Women are always afraid of a revolt starting up. My mother, may she rest in peace, couldn't bear to have any Negroes in the house. My father had to employ a British staff. When the next bad year for cotton came along, my father took pleasure in sending that staff away. So there's been no trouble at all here, then."

"Nothing serious, Miss Grace. A little ruckus in the black church can hardly start up a full-scale revolt."

"What do you mean by a 'ruckus', Jack?" Miss Grace was alert. "A fight, for instance?"

"Just an argument. One of the boys wanted to get married and the preacher wouldn't do it on account of not having your permission in writing. That's all it comes to."

"Was my permission asked for? I wouldn't hesitate about a thing like that. It's the sort of incident that could blow up out of all proportion."

"These two wanted to get married on short notice." Jack Ryder shrugged. "It would be hard to take them seriously, Miss Grace. They just know each other for a few days and they want to get married. Why, there are times when I don't understand them. Marriage means nothing to them. They just want to feel more at ease about the sins they're already committing, if you'll pardon my saying so."

Grace Parker stood up by way of dismissing the overseer. The little incident hadn't been important

72

after all. There was a clatter of noise on the stairs as Eli Crosby started down them, and the noise propelled Ryder to his feet as nothing else might have done. He had spent most of last night drinking himself into a stupor, and the after-effects lingered on.

"It does seem strange, that kind of behavior," Grace Parker said as he stood up. "But I'm glad you mentioned it all the same. Let the slaves know that if permission is asked for it'll be given."

"Yes, Miss Grace," Jack Ryder said, putting the glass on a coaster as he got up. "I heard the story from Rufus, my best driver. He's got it in for the new boy and he passed it on. I use my sources of information when they're needed, Miss Grace, and always keep my lines open, so to speak."

Instead of giving praise for the pains that he took as part of the job, Miss Grace seemed rigid.

"The new boy did you say? Sebastian?"

"That's his name, yes. Talks like he has a meat-grinder in his mouth and is always puttin' on airs."

Miss Grace suddenly sat down again. Ryder, reaching thankfully for what was left of his drink, was going to sit back in the chair he liked so much, but she said softly:

"You can go now, Mr. Ryder."

She had closed her eyes and gripped the chair arms as if for dear life. Ryder shrugged, said something polite, and returned to his cabin for a little solitary drinking. On the way he walked over to the female slave cabin and brought back a pretty gal. She was called Annabel, and smiled sweetly in spite of having only two teeth in her mouth. Whenever Annabel smiled Ryder remembered the old slave called Mose, who pulled the teeth of slaves if they had any complaint in the dental way. In the case of Annabel, it seemed, Mose must have gone too far.

He was in bed with Annabel, watching her make love to him, his hands extended down to her shoulders, when a series of urgent knocks sounded on his door . . .

Left alone, Grace Parker seethed quietly. She couldn't keep from thinking about the damnable nerve of that Northern nigger who hadn't been able to do anything with her because he was doing it all with some slave gal. It was all right if he picked one of his own after a while, but not at Rootstock. And he certainly didn't plan on staying a slave for the rest of his life.

Simply by knowing somebody else as well as he knew that slave gal, it stood to reason that sooner or later he would tell her what he had done with Grace Parker. Then all the slaves would know about it! *All* the slaves!

It had to be stopped! She must get Sebastian away from Rootstock as soon as possible.

Grace wasn't able to concentrate because of the noises at the stairwell, and she realized that she ought to go out and bid her guest farewell. She muttered under her breath as she left the parlor, her mind on the problem of getting rid of Sebastian.

Eli Crosby had reached the bottom step. He had managed to shave, but his eyes were bloodshot and his nose was glowing like a beacon. His clothes looked rumpled on the chunky figure that moved shakily as if he was in a gale.

"I seem to have made an abysmal nuisance of myself last night," he said, smiling to add to his apology.

"It wasn't entirely your fault," she said, her mind miles away. She suddenly looked at him as if she had never seen him before, eyes wide in wonder, lips parted, head cocked to one side. "Eli, would you let me prevail on you to join me in the parlor for a moment?"

He lumbered after her, as if every nerve in his body wasn't screaming to get back to Haven. Grace had cleared away Jack Ryder's drinking glass, but

74

Eli Crosby refused to sit and shuddered at the notion of taking a drink. He stood up and swayed perilously back and forth.

"Do you remember saying that you wanted a boy of mine?" she asked, not showing annoyance at having to look up at him. "A Northern boy named Sebastian."

"Yes." Eli Crosby made and unmade fists. "I have a score to settle with that Sebastian of yours."

"Well, you can have the boy if you still want him."

"I do, yes," Eli Crosby said promptly. "But I can't help wondering . . . you made him a house boy and now you're getting rid of him." He flushed to the roots of his hair at one withering look from her. "I beg your pardon."

"I'll tell one of the house slaves to ask Mr. Ryder to come back," she said coolly, "and Mr. Ryder will see to it that Sebastian comes to the house. After that, Eli, he is in your hands."

There wasn't a house slave in sight, this being Sunday, and she had to ask Blossom, the cook, to search out Mr. Ryder. The overseer was back at the main house in twenty minutes. He nodded at the message to bring Sebastian up to the house, then left and sent for Rufus. The best driver was ordered to take Sebastian to the overseer's cabin. Ryder would then escort Sebastian to the main house.

In the parlor again, Grace sat down and closed her eyes to indicate that she didn't want any more talk with Eli Crosby. The owner of Haven, though, was not to be denied.

"Has this Sebastian made you any trouble?" Eli probed. "Has he tried to touch you? Rape you, maybe?"

She said nothing.

"Was it more serious than trying to touch you?" Eli demanded. "Did he attack you? Did he make a try at rape?"

Grace wouldn't talk to him, no matter what he might think. Let him give Sebastian a hard time.

Ominously he said, "You don't have to answer any more, Grace. Your silence spoke for you."

Her eyes flew open. "I didn't mean for you to think—"

"Originally, I had figured to whip him and turn him free. He was technically free in the first place," Crosby said. "After what you just told me, Grace, I'm duty bound to protect your honor."

"How?" Grace asked hoarsely. "What will you do?"

"Why, Grace, I'm going to hang that boy."

Chapter Six

Sebastian was taken to the main house by Jack Ryder. He wasn't able to put on house slippers or change into his house boy's outfit. He supposed that Grace Parker was entertaining somebody today as well and wanted him to do some work.

Not till he was taken into the parlor and the door was closed on him did he know that he was in trouble.

Eli Crosby asked, "You got any last words, boy?"

Sebastian knew just how bad this situation had become. He had heard about this sort of thing happening in the South, but had never believed it. In one swift second, he believed everything.

He heard some treads outside, in the hall, but supposed that the old wooden planks were groaning after having been used. Nobody else appeared to have heard and he told himself it didn't matter.

Eli Crosby said to the overseer, "Leave me that dog whip of yours and get a rope."

Ryder kept a hangman's rope in his cabin, but woudn't let on that the problem was such an easy one for him to solve. He had tried to get praise last time for doing his work well, but Miss Grace ignored him. Now she'd pay for that.

"I'll see if I can find a rope," he said, making his voice sound as if he doubted such a thing had ever existed on earth.

He went slowly to his cabin, got a pair of drinks under his belt, drew out the hangman's rope, washed his mouth with water, and then hurried to the main house again.

His appearance with the rope made Miss Grace shudder. Nobody else in the room seemed to have moved, but a pair of fresh welts had appeared on the nigger's chest.

"There's a big tree past the main house," Eli Crosby said. "We can use that for the job."

"Good." Jack Ryder nodded. "I'll leave the body up for a few days so that the other niggers can see what happens if they don't do the work they're told."

Grace Parker leaned forward. "I don't think you'll be able to hang him at all," she said carefully. "There's something you've forgotten."

Blossom, the cook, was trembling in her agitation. She was a big woman and a fine cook, as her mother and grandmother had been before her. But cooking was the last thing on her mind at the moment.

She had been sent to bring Mister Jack over to the house again and had heard one of the gals in the cabin with him, come to think of it. Not that it mattered, but a little while had passed until Mister Jack returned. Remembering that Miss Grace had looked so excited and worried, Blossom had listened at the parlor door and had heard about plans to lynch the new buck with the lah-di-dah manners.

Blossom would have been upset, of course, at the notion of any lynching, but she liked Sebastian more than most. His smile at her was a sure sign that she was still a good-looking gal and could still get some play from a man. Sebastian hadn't really done anything more to make her feel like that, but he never could help making an impression on a woman.

As Blossom stood in center-kitchen, eyes closed and praying silently, a door opened at the rear of the house. She reached for a rolling pin almost before she knew what she was doing. She put the pin down, knowing very well that she couldn't do anything to stop a lynching if the whites had made up their minds to it.

She had seen one lynching in the past, and would

never forget the sight of that dead boy, his eyes bulging and his hands frantically trying to ease the pressure of the rope biting into his neck. He had died that way, with hands clawing at the rope, and the body had been shown to the slaves for a week afterwards.

The slaves got pretty restless and mad on account of what had happened, though, and the body had to be cut down and most of the slaves sold someplace else. Blossom happened to be a good cook, so Miss Grace's daddy hadn't sold her.

She rushed out to see who was coming in by the back entrance to the main house. She had half-hoped it would be some big strapping boy like Rufus who might dig in his spurs and try to help Sebastian in some way. But it was only Alfred, the tidyminded house slave who was Miss Grace's butler.

He nodded at her and started for the rear stairs.

Blossom asked, open-mouthed, "You—you can't have come out here today to help him?"

"I've come over to get some extra work done on the guest rooms and save myself having to do it to-morrow," Alfred said vigorously. "If I don't do it, nobody going to come in and do it for me."

When the whites used words like "lazy nigger" they certainly didn't mean Alfred.

Blossom drew a forefinger across her lips for him to keep quieter, at least, then gestured him into the kitchen. He stood with legs apart and hands behind his back while she talked. He closed his eyes tightly for a while, and his jaw was set when he opened them again.

"Where is Sebastian now?"

"In the house with Mr. Crosby and Miss Grace and Jack Ryder. All of them are in the parlor.

"No lynchings," he said softly. "No more lynchings."

Then he turned and ran out of the kitchen and the house, going toward the slave pens.

81

Alfred started to call out for the slaves to gather round him, but he had run so fast he couldn't talk. One or two surprised-looking slaves did run to the pens to join him, and Alfred realized that they had been drawn by sight of his butler outfit, rather than the usual slave-pen rags he wore over here. The clothes drew a crowd for him, but he had to waste more time catching his breath. In spite of his tautness and gasping, he managed to stand out of reach of the boys who wanted to touch the expensive clothing.

"Lynch," he said, getting the most important word out first. "It hasn't happened yet, but it's going to. They'll be lynching Sebastian."

Rufus, who had been in the foreground with the other questioners, suddenly made a move to get out of the circle, which grew wider as his friends started to leave with the huge slave.

"Don't you care, Rufus?" Alfred asked.

The slave shrugged. "Did I know what the whites wanted, I'd 'a hanged him myself."

Somebody in the crowd drew a deep breath of anger, and Rufus knew he had lost the sympathy of some slaves. He shrugged it off irritably.

Alfred said, "If a lot of us go over to the main house, they'll know we can give 'em trouble over any lynching."

"Are you crazy, old man?" somebody demanded. "Why should they care if we get mad?"

"After a lynching there's generally trouble for months afterwards and whites know it," Alfred said stubbornly. "A lot of boys try to run away and there's more thieving."

"The whites just have to say he's been sold to Eli Crosby and that's the last we hear about another rope-dancing nigger."

Alfred, surprised at his own firmness, said, "Then we don't let Crosby take him."

82

"So Mister Jack Ryder cuts into all of us with whips and then Sebastian gets taken away."

"If Miss Grace has a lot of troublemaking slaves on her hands, she needs to get rid of 'em and she can't afford to sell so many good slaves and buy others who she don't know nothing about. Once we go over to the main house, we've got what we want."

Rufus heard the crowd muttering around him and knew that a number of slaves would certainly be in front of the main house. If they got what they wanted and Rufus had been too scared to be with them, he would never hear the last of it from any of them. Worse yet, nobody was ever again going to think of him as a natural leader.

"I can handle it myself," Rufus said, swaggering. "There doesn't anybody have to come with me."

Alfred realized that the big slave would probably go anywhere in Rootstock rather than to the main building if he was left to himself. Later on, he could say that Sebastian had been sold and that would be the end of any trouble as far as he was concerned.

He said, "We all want to come with you, Rufus, and we know you're the best for the job."

"Come on, then," Rufus said. "Come on then, every one of you. Hurry up."

The word was passed along quickly. Slaves were interrupted at eating and sleeping, at lazing around; and one gal's dress was hiked up when she first came running into sight, so that the slaves knew what she had been doing. Nobody chuckled or laughed, not at a time like this.

Orchid had appeared at Alfred's side. The pert little slave gal, eyes downcast, walked side by side with the house slave as the largely silent crowd started for the main house.

Eli Crosby was trying to be patient. His head was near to bursting after last night's drinking ructions and his attempt to sleep it off at Rootstock, but at the very notion of a lynching he had snapped back to attention.

"Grace, I can't understand why you're being so stubborn," he said. "We're getting rid of the boy if you like it right now or you don't."

"You can't hang him at all," she said. "He's a free man. He's nobody's property. If you hang him in front of witnesses, you can be sent to prison."

"Slave witnesses couldn't testify in a court."

"*I* could testify."

Eli Crosby said, "All I want is to make it up to you for what happened and for that to be an example to other niggers."

Jack Ryder was scowling. "There's nothing like a lynching to get the others riled up, Mr. Crosby. I'll have a lot of trouble keeping them in line afterwards."

"We'll take him to my place, then," Eli Crosby said. "We'll do the job at Haven. I've got an overseer who knows enough to keep his niggers in line."

Jack Ryder flushed, but didn't make any comment. He had realized at last that Miss Grace didn't want any harm coming to the boy and would do his best to keep it from happening.

Sebastian had been watching as if this was a bad play and he had only got mixed up in it as one of the actors. He couldn't make himself believe that any of this was happening to him.

From behind, Eli Crosby suddenly pushed him. He had to keep from turning on Crosby, which was probably what the man had been hoping for. It would show clearly that Sebastian wasn't worth keeping alive, as he didn't know his place.

What Sebastian did instead was to behave as if he had been pushed hard enough to lose his balance. He fell against the window, careful to keep from breaking it. The window was partly open and he made a try to see if it could be pushed open further

84

in the counterclockwise way. He had to do it quietly, while covering the moves with his body and drooping as if he had been hurt. Let the window open and it could take him out of here.

The window wouldn't budge.

From the corner of an eye he saw the slaves coming toward the main house. They looked grim-faced, all of them. He didn't believe his eyes, but stared at the long ragged line of Negro faces.

Eli Crosby was saying to the overseer, "Ryder, you'll help get this into the carriage."

Grace Parker said, "You'll stay here with me, Jack."

"If you want to do what you know is right, you've got a job waiting for you at Haven," Eli Crosby said firmly. "That's a promise, and a gentleman's word is always good as gold—hey! Get the nigger away from that window."

Sebastian tried to push the window as hard as he was able, but it didn't give more than half an inch. Ryder lumbered over to him and reached out a hand, but Sebastian ducked under it. Ryder's hard hand smashed part of the window glass, which gave with a deafening roar.

Outside somebody called out, "He's there! Behind that broken glass!"

Orchid's voice was raised, "Sebastian, it's me, Sebastian!"

Frantically, Sebastian worked at the window. Ryder rubbed one hand hard against the other, trying to ease the pain. It was Eli Crosby who stopped Sebastian by drawing out a pistol from beneath his jacket.

"Get away from there, nigger, if you don't want lead weights in you when you get lynched."

There was no choice. The man could kill him by twitching his right forefinger; he didn't have to touch Sebastian at all. It would be so much easier for him this way. Sebastian moved from the window.

"All right, now walk real slow over to the door," Crosby started. "You're coming to Haven and going straight up a rope when you get there. Ryder, give me that rope if you can't nerve yourself to do what a man has to do and come along with m—what's the matter with you, Ryder? And you, too, Grace. Both of you look like a pair of sick sheep."

Grace Parker had walked to the window. She turned around to face him, then suddenly stepped to one side.

Eli glanced out the shattered window at the angry line of black faces. He snorted. "The pistol will attend to any troublemakers."

"And afterwards I'll have trouble from the survivors."

"Sell them," Crosby snapped. "I'll take any you want and give you just as many in good condition. You can trade, if you'd rather."

"I'd have to trade all of them and it would take months to get started up again," she said. "That cat won't jump."

Crosby raised the pistol, aiming at Sebastian's heart.

Grace said, "The noise will send all those blacks roaring in here and you haven't got enough bullets in that pistol to take care of them all."

"Ryder's got a dog whip for the ones I don't send up to Heaven."

"He can't whip a hundred blacks at the same time," Grace snapped, her face chalky.

"Grace I won't rest unt—wait! I've got the answer." A wicked glint appeared in his pig eyes as he turned to the overseer. "Are you with me, Ryder?"

"Well, I can't use the rope because both my hands aren't good as they ought to be. I really got hurt on that window."

"Miss Grace will help you," Crosby said, grinning. "Otherwise, the truth about a very nasty incident is likely to get around to all of our mutual

86

friends and she won't enjoy her life too much afterwards." He smiled. "I think that'll do it."

Grace closed her eyes tightly, but said nothing.

Ryder, still nursing his wounded hand, asked harshly, "What's this plan of yours?"

"Hang him in the house itself," Eli Crosby said.

Grace put in strongly, "I'd burn it down afterwards. Do you think I could stand to look every day at the place where some black boy was lynched?"

"You don't go into the cellar very often, Grace, do you?" Eli Crosby smiled. "Well, that's where we'll get it done."

Grace stared at the man who was obsessed with blood and death, the man she had known well for so many years.

Crosby flicked a glance toward Sebastian. "Come on, boy. You've got yourself a very important appointment and there isn't any time to spare."

The slaves stood sullenly in front of the main house, Rufus in front of the jagged line. Not a word was spoken by anybody at first.

Sam, a friend of his, asked quietly, "Why don't we do something else? I say we go in."

Rufus stared at him. "And I say you keep your mouth closed tight, nigger!"

Alfred, who had been looking in sympathy at Orchid, glanced over at Sam. "You listen to Rufus and do what he says. Rufus knows best."

The big slave smiled. Alfred turned back to Orchid again, hoping that his fulsome flattery could keep the big slave from any violent moves.

"The Lord knows what might happen," Blossom said loudly, having joined them from the house. She had drawn a scarf around her ample shoulders for the cool of the Georgia late afternoon. "The Lord will provide."

The loudness of her voice was followed by Jack

Ryder's pushing his black-haired head out the shattered window, which had been half-opened first for him to look out.

"I can see you, Blossom," he called. "And Alfred. House jobs only go to good niggers who do what they're told, so I'm telling you both to get away from there."

Blossom squared her shoulders but didn't move. Alfred glanced at slaves who were slinking away.

Rufus made a turn, whether to pull one of the slaves back or get away himself he would never know.

The motion caught Ryder's eye, though. "Don't think I can't make you out, too, Rufus. And don't think I can't get myself some new drivers, either.

The big slave stood quietly, hands made into fists.

"All right," he said, eyes slitted with anger. "If I'm in trouble, we all are."

Blossom said fervently, "That's right, boy. We're all in it together."

Rufus hadn't been understood, it seemed. He glanced up to see that the overseer had pulled his head back inside, then said, "The whites are in trouble, too. I take no sass from black or white."

"Take your ease, boy," Alfred said, sensing the big slave's actual mood. "We're doing what we can."

"What *you* can, old man," Rufus shouted. One or two slaves suddenly ran off back to the slave pens. They would stay on their straw pallets for the next few hours, hands clapped over their ears as they rocked back and forth and prayed.

Orchid forced her big eyes away from the house where her man was being held a prisoner. "You'll kill him if you try and fight them."

Rufus stopped himself from saying that he didn't care what happened to Sebastian. "That fellow of yours was the one who told us about them early Hebrews who stood up against slavery. If they could do it, we can. I say we do it right now!"

A cheer went up from the crowd, but nobody would move toward the house. Rufus took a dozen steps in the direction of the house, looked back scornfully, then picked up a rock and threw it at the nearest window. It landed, and glass shards glittered in the weakening sun before they flew off in all directions.

Rufus ran toward the house entrance and began battering his big body against the closed back door. That was when Sam, his friend, hurried to join him. A few other slaves, who had hesitated at first, hurried after Sam.

A half dozen male slaves started to shout with pleasure at the notion of what they expected would be happening very soon. Some of them picked up rocks and hurled them at windows, two of which suddenly were smashed to pieces.

"Don't break yourselves on the door," one of the slaves called out. "Go in through a window."

Rufus, who had nearly splintered the door in his urge to destroy, knew that only a few more attacks would force the door to cave in. He found himself deserted by Sam and the others, though. Like them, he clambered in by one of the windows, but his first move when inside was to unlock the rear door and then smash the lock with a chair.

Chapter Seven

The cellar was cold and damp. Sebastian, who had been guided here by the pistol of Eli Crosby, was breathing with difficulty. The air was moldy, but his nostrils sucked it up eagerly because he wouldn't be able to breathe at all in a little while when Eli Crosby finally had his way.

He was starting to feel sorry for himself. It could keep him from thinking clearly. Besides, he had never acted a death scene and it seemed a little unfair for an actor to die without having rehearsed it.

Eli Crosby's face was bland, except for a sheen of sweat around the eyes. He was certainly enjoying himself.

"Cover him with that whip of yours," Crosby told the overseer, "while I get the fixings all ready."

Grace Parker glared at the overseer, who swallowed and then apologized.

"Miss Grace, no matter what you think about the rights and wrongs of it, Mr. Crosby has got the pistol and that's good enough for me. One thing you learn in this world is never to monkey around with the man who carries the gun."

Grace Parker kept glaring at her overseer, but she said nothing.

Crosby tied the rope at one end against a wooden beam close to the cellar ceiling. He stretched the rope down and it reached the floor and coiled around a few times. He had to work hard and patiently to knot the rope into a circle above his own head.

"Get a chair," he ordered Grace. "Get it for me, I say."

She wouldn't move. Ryder taking only a step away from Sebastian, kicked a chair across to Eli Crosby. The chair fell and Crosby had to pick it up, letting go the rope so that it fell to the floor again.

93

Finally, the job was done. The hangman's rope was made, the noose ready for Sebastian.

"You," Crosby snapped at Sebastian. "Get up on that chair if you don't want your kneecaps full of lead first. I won't hesitate, and it hurts like hell in the kneecap."

"Hanging hurts worse," Sebastian said from a dry throat. He didn't move.

Crosby snarled and raised the pistol.

Carefully, without a wasted motion, Grace stepped in front of the black man so that she was standing between Sebastian and the pistol.

"You'll have to shoot me first," she said.

Sebastian whirled around on Ryder, trying to guess his chances at taking the whip out of the man's good hand. Now that there was a shield, he might be able to do it.

He had actually taken a step in that direction when Crosby moved. The Southern gentleman punched Grace in the side of the jaw. The punch sounded like a hammer striking ice under a wet rag. Grace reeled and fell heavily.

The overseer drew a deep pained breath, almost as if he himself had been hit, and hurried over to help Grace Parker to her feet.

"On that chair, coon," Eli Crosby snapped. The pistol muzzle was aimed directly at Sebastian's left kneecap.

Sebastian glanced across at Ryder to see that the man was busy. Making believe he was following Crosby's orders and slowly going toward the chair, he suddenly whirled on the white man. Not long ago he had done Eli Crosby some damage, and he could certainly do it again.

He put both hands on Crosby's pistol arm, forcing the weapon up and aside where it wouldn't fire on him. When he withdrew one hand to punch Crosby, the pistol was brought halfway back to where it had been so that it was aimed at his side.

94

Sebastian raised a foot, kicking Crosby between the legs. The plantation owner fell back, gasping and cursing, but the space between them gave him a chance to raise the pistol. It was pointed at him again when all of them heard the sound of glass being shattered.

Grace Parker suddenly raised her voice and screamed, "We're in the cellar! Come to the cellar!"

"You fool woman," Crosby snarled. "Do you want them after you?"

Bare-footed slaves hurried around over their heads. There was some trouble with a rear door.

"If the two of you have got any brains, you'll finish the job I started," Crosby said suddenly, turning away from the knotted rope. "I have to get help and I'll need all the bullets I've got. Using one on this buck would be a waste."

He moved to the cellar door as quickly as he could. Grace, upright and rigid in spite of the bruise at the right side of her jaw, laughed shortly.

Ryder shouted, "If you don't take me and Miss Grace with you, we're dead."

Crosby may have heard, but he didn't stop.

Grace smiled at Sebastian. "I'll bet you've never seen white people frightened before this, have you?"

Ryder scowled and raised the dog whip in his hand.

Above them, the noises grew louder.

Eli Crosby left the cellar and started for the stairs. He had taken a step or two up the wooden stairs, pistols at the ready, when he heard one of the slaves shout:

"White man over here!"

And another, a woman, shouted, "Let's kill him."

Rather than use up bullets he might need, Crosby plunged down the stairs, losing balance in his hurry. He fell against a section of wood that gave. It had been a door. He thanked his lucky stars and looked out. There wasn't a nigger in sight. He ran.

His carriage had been slightly removed from the main entrance, so he headed for it and scrambled into the back seat. He was gasping for breath.

"Drive, you black fool," he called out toward the coachman's place. "Drive!"

The carriage stood still. His black fool of a coachman had joined the others.

Crosby, breathing hard, clambered out of the carriage and up to the trap, a painted wooden board on which the coachman sat when he was driving. The horses had become restless on account of noises from the house.

Crosby's first touch on the reins set them off luckily, but in the whirling kaleidoscope that flashed by at his sides he soon realized that the horses were moving in the direction they wanted to take rather than that in which Crosby wanted to take them. He realized, too, that the horses were taking him in a large circle.

He had never worked so hard in his life or felt more of a fool doing it. The horses wouldn't do what he wanted. Crosby finally balanced himself somehow in the whirling carriage, then drew out his pistol and fired off a snap shot.

The horses no longer moved in a circle, but they ran out of control. As they moved away from the cursed grounds back of him, Crosby sighed and wondered how much longer it would take before he was able to get help for Grace Parker. Not for a moment did he doubt that she was in trouble, and he certainly didn't want any white person killed by a bunch of marauding niggers.

Besides, he had every intention of leading the group of whites who would come back with him to Rootstock, where they would punish each and every one of the slaves who had taken part in this insurrection.

96

He supposed he might have taken Grace along with him, but it had been hard enough for one person to escape—let alone a man and a woman and an idiot overseer as well.

Did he *want* something bad to happen to Grace, though, after all? Did he want an excuse for seeing those slaves punished worse than they might be, otherwise? Was he willing to let Grace Parker lose her life so he could feed his animal appetites for vengeance? It couldn't be!

All the same, he had to be the one who brought help to Grace Parker. Nobody else would be able to do it!

He had been abstracted for too long a time. The horses had started along a rocky path that wasn't any part of a road. Crosby tried to divert the frenzied animals, having glanced back to make sure that he was far from Rootstock no matter what happened. He cursed at the idiot horses, but it did no good. They were headed for a mound of rocks and Crosby had lost control of the reins for whatever good that might have done him; the bumpy path had simply been enough to make the reins jump out of his hand, it seemed. He turned to jump out, but it was too late. The horses charged that rock mo nd, destroying themselves and tumbling the carriage down a steep, wide path. Eli Crosby blacked out before the carriage struck the ground.

In the big house, the main house, the pride and joy of several generations of the Parker family, slaves started to wreak their vengeance.

"What's this?" a slave girl asked.

"It looks like a piece of you-know-what on a string."

"Watch your mouth, you! Know what it is? It's a kind of thing as gets knitted."

"Rip it up, honey. Miss Grace ain't gonna need it."

"Maybe I can take it with me."

He picked up the knitwear and tried to rip it across. It wouldn't rip. Angrily he dropped it, then kicked it into the fireplace.

"She won't miss it and you won't need it," he snapped. "Get me that heavy thing over there, so I can break this window. I show 'em all, that's what I do."

Outside, in front of the house, Orchid asked fearfully, "What can we do now?"

Blossom pursed her lips. Shrugging the scarf more tightly around her shoulders even the late afternoon has turned a little warmer in the last few minutes, the cook said:

"We can pray, honey."

"Is that all?"

"Is that all?"

"If you do it right, honey, it's enough."

In a side room one of the male slaves modeled a dress in the mirror, his soft-featured face crinkling into a warm smile as the dress draped his figure.

"Ain't this beautiful, darling?"

His long-time friend, Jethro, gave a snort of disgust. "Don't you get tired of lookin' at yourself so much time?"

"I'm just beginning. I'll take the looking-glass with me and the dress, too, and I'd like to see you stop me."

"Sure, you take it. Soon as this ruckus is over, the whites search the pens and find it and you're finished."

In the main dining room, three slaves turned the table upside down and ran into the kitchen for elaborate dishes. They cracked them across the upside-down table legs.

"Ain't this fun?" a slave asked. He could hardly

98

make himself heard above the noise of cracking dishes.

He threw a plate toward one of the others. That slave, not expecting it, was hit lightly on the chin. He called out furiously, lurched toward the slave who tried to hit him and then picked up a teacup and threw that. It hit the first slave, who threw back a saucer. The third slave, caught in the middle, started throwing the stack of dishes in front of him. The slaves were soon bruising themselves by breaking dishes against each other.

In the kitchen a slave named Aristotle poured wine from different bottles into fragile glasses. He sniffed, winced, turned to the girl next to him and broke two bottles.

"You know what, baby?" he asked, reaching for the nearest slave girl. "You taste a lot better. Come over here and let me taste you."

In spite of the furious noises all around them, Aristotle and his gal made love. Never had they enjoyed it more.

The sounds of destruction could be heard by the three slaves who had remained outside. Alfred winced, then set his jaw firmly and drew a deep breath that was almost a sob. Blossom sighed. Orchid had been standing at Alfred's side, her eyes widening as she listened and saw an occasional window being smashed and heard gleeful shouts.

"Praying isn't good enough," she said, looking directly at the cook. A sob was torn from her throat. "I won't stay out here while my man is inside dying."

She broke loose from Alfred's gentle touch and ran toward the main house.

Blossom said urgently, "She'll be slaughtered in there."

"I'll go after her." Alfred swallowed air. It was

the last thing he wanted to do now. "You'd best stay in the slave pens until this is played out. Whoever keeps alive after this, Blossom, is gonna need a good cook."

His little smile disappeared when he turned away and half-walked, half-ran to the main house, following Orchid as best he could.

Rufus didn't try to stop the others from making noises while they smashed up whatever they liked. They could let out a little steam and Rufus would be able to do the thing that he wanted to.

The others might destroy furniture and clothes and smash windows and walls and make love in the ruins, but Rufus wanted to destroy people . . . white people.

He went from one room to another. A boy and gal were making love, a trio of slaves were throwing things at each other, one boy was crooning to another one. Wine bottles had been smashed and their insides spilled. The fireplace was choked with things to be burned by slaves who chortled as they did their work. There wasn't one white person in sight, though, damn it. Not one.

He ran up the stairs and into the pens where the whites were supposed to sleep. Every white person slept on a soft bed in a clean room. There was one bed in each room, and most of the beds were so narrow that it didn't seem as if more than one white could sleep in it. Some of the beds had already been smashed by slaves who were going from room to room. The bedheads had been kicked in, the mattresses overturned. One mattress had been thrown out of a window. Every mirror in sight had been broken.

There wasn't one white person upstairs, either, but Rufus was so busy making sure about it that he almost didn't hear Sam's shout from below.

"White man over here!" Sam shouted.

Some gals shouted back a few words about killing him. Rufus nearly jumped the flight of round curving stairs. Two slaves had been working to smash the steps with twin hammers, stamping on the polished wood as soon as there was a dent in it. Rufus very nearly caught both hammers with his feet.

Sam wasn't in sight on the first floor. The staircase leading to the cellar wasn't near him and he had to run around like a chicken with his head off until he found the damn stairs. Nobody had ruined those stairs yet, so he ran down without difficulty. Sam was kicking an opened door with his feet and the door was letting weak sunshine into the cellar.

"White bastard ran out before I could catch him," Sam said fiercely.

"There've got to be others," Rufus said, determinedly. "Where's *she?*"

"Miss Grace, you mean?"

"The white bitch is who I mean."

Sam looked nervously up and down the short hallway.

"There is nobody to be afraid of any more," Rufus said, and Sam recoiled at the wave of hate flowing from his friend. "What's more, you can have seconds when I get done, and she won't be the last white bitch we get ourselves."

Sam's brow was furrowed. "Wouldn't she talk about it? Miss Grace, I mean."

"She'll talk in hell," Rufus said, "because that's where we send her after I get finished. After *you* get finished, I ought to say." He smiled. "Scared, boy?"

Sam puffed himself up, growing taller as Rufus looked. "There isn't nothing you know about as could scare me."

Rufus had started walking the hallway. He found a door and pushed against it, but it wouldn't budge.

"It's locked so tight that you can bet the white bitch is back of it," he said, and turned away briefly.

"Run upstairs and get the best battering-ram you can find. Push it down the stairs if you want, but don't stop for anything else except that ram. And hurry! I've got the itch and I've got it real bad."

Chapter Eight

Eli Crosby was sputtering and coughing when he came to consciousness again. Hot, dark liquid seemed to have been smeared against his lips, a touch convinced him through bleary eyes. It was drawing towards evening, and he wasn't more than fifty feet from the scene of the accident.

A rough looking man in farmer's clothes stood over him. In one hand he held a bottle with dark liquid in it.

"Figured you'd come around after a dose of blue lightning," the farmer said. "Wakes up the dead, it does."

Crosby sat up and tried to look out toward Rootstock. He felt guilty for leaving and guilty for having brought on the trouble and guilty because he was crazy for Grace Parker and hated her guts at the same time.

The farmer said, "Your carriage and horses didn't make it, mister. Sorry."

Crosby spoke carefully. "You've got to take me to the nearest big plantation. It's very important."

The farmer scratched his jaw. He was a young fellow in the thirties, not a quick thinker.

"Nearest would be Rootstock," he said. "Miss Grace Parker's place."

"No, I mean beside that. And not Haven, either."

"It would be closer to take you into town," the farmer said, gesturing to his right. "All I'd have to do is cut across those fields and join the splinter road just past them. A whole raft of plantations on the other side."

It was true enough. Crosby nodded.

"Into town, then." He managed to lift himself to his feet and was halfway to the farmer's empty hay wagon before the young fellow had finished inviting him into it. In spite of injuries and dizziness he clambered up to the wooden buckboard without help. The farmer, who gave his name as Sharp, followed slowly enough to convince Crosby that he had been misnamed. Crosby had to keep from taking the driver's seat impatiently.

The drive was slow and whenever Crosby talked, the farmer would stop gentling his horses. Crosby learned to keep quiet.

"Why not take me to the constable's house?" he asked finally, when the cluster of houses in town suddenly came into sight. He can round up the men I need."

"Constable?" Sharp was patient. "Had I known you wanted him, I'd have come into town from the other side."

Crosby kept from saying that all he wanted was somebody who would know that there was an emergency at Rootstock, if it wasn't asking for too much.

The constable lived in the jail house, which was a small brick building with bars at the windows. There was no response to his first knocks, so he began pounding vigorously with his fists.

"What do you want?" a thick-tongued voice demanded. A heavy-featured man had poked his head out of a second floor window. "The constable's over to Clara's place, and I've got some hard drinking to sleep off."

Crosby was relieved that the man wasn't the constable. He was annoyed to see the establishment being run in such a slipshod way.

Crosby turned away, but the bumbling farmer, Sharp, had taken himself and his wagon out of the neighborhood.

The Tremont tavern was open, and the bartender winkingly told him that Miss Clara's place was the last house at the end of the street.

He was knocking at the door of Miss Clara's place in a few minutes. A hard-looking woman in

106

her forties came to the door and stood with hands on hips.

"I want to talk to the constable instantly," Crosby said. "It's a matter of law and order."

Miss Clara recognized wealth when she saw it. She drew back and gestured to a door at the far end of the long hall, which was furnished with mirrors and paintings and smelled of perfume. The wallpaper was in deep red.

Crosby knocked twice on the sturdy door that had been pointed out to him. "Constable, you're wanted. It's urgent, life and death."

There was a sound of giggling from inside the room, but nobody moved. Crosby pounded several more times. A few other doors in the hallway opened and some men and women looked out angrily, but nothing happened behind the constable's door that was of any help to Crosby. Or to Grace Parker, for that matter.

Finally, there was a long gasp from a man's throat. Crosby, who had taken to kicking the door and cursing furiously, brushed Miss Clara aside when the madam tried to stop him.

Soft footsteps could be heard on the other side of the door. It opened on a young red-haired girl in her twenties. She wore a shift which had been put on hastily.

Crosby opened the door wider and walked into the room. On the bed he saw a Negro gal, pretty and looking at peace with the world. Over to one side at a basin, a heavy man was briskly washing himself.

"Constable, are you ready to do your job?"

The constable gestured for Crosby to keep talking.

Crosby said sarcastically, "I'd prefer to talk alone."

Crosby held the door open while he watched the girls walk out of earshot. The constable was washing

107

with soap and water. He finally wiped his face with a clean towel, then turned around.

"I declare that I don't know what gets into me sometimes," he sighed. "And with a nigger gal, too."

Crosby finally closed the door. "There's been a slave revolt at Rootstock," he said briskly. "Miss Grace Parker's honor and life are at stake and some men have to get to Rootstock to crush the niggers once and for all. I'll be glad to go back, but I can't do it alone."

The constable, who had been about to part his hair in the center, suddenly whirled around and made for the front door.

"Come on, man," he called back over a shoulder. "This is no time to dawdle."

"But what are you going to do?"

"Do?" the constable shouted. "Get us some good men and we'll get out to Rootstock and you can be damn sure we'll all send those slaves to hell."

Rufus led the way as he and Sam crashed into the cellar. The door opened so quickly that Rufus, off-balance, was hurled part of the way across the huge, drafty room. He heard a whip crack while he was trying to get his balance and not till he was straight did he realize that the whip hadn't touched him.

The whip was in Jack Ryder's right hand. The overseer's face was gray and there was almost a touch of blackness under the lips but above the chin. At his side, rigid with anger, stood Grace Parker. Behind them, watching the others, was Sebastian. There was a rope with a hangman's noose and a rickety chair under it.

Rufus swaggered and said to Sebastian, "We came to set you free, boy, and that's a trick you couldn't turn by yourself."

Sebastian didn't look grateful, even though he must have spent a hellish time here with the others.

108

But Rufus had spoken in such a way that nobody with self-respect could feel anything but resentment.

For the first time Rufus looked Grace Parker up and down as if he had never seen her before. His eyes rested on the sight of her breasts through the dress.

"I'll get to you later, gal," he drawled insolently.

He wanted to see Grace Parker's response to that, of course, but she didn't seem to move or change in any way.

Jack Ryder said sharply, "Get out, Rufus, or you'll be whipped half to death. Which is it to be?"

But Rufus, although he looked away from Grace Parker, was still smiling insolently. He was shaking his head now, too. His lower lip curled contemptuously.

"That cat won't jump," he said. Ryder's face flushed. "This black boy doesn't move any more just because you *say* for him to move."

Ryder said thinly, "I can't be sure how long I'll be able to control myself, Rufus. Get out."

"You've got the whip in your hand. Why not go ahead and use it?"

"Get out," Ryder said again, his voice rising.

Rufus shook his head. "One of us is going to die right now."

Nobody in the cellar expected to see such cat-quickness as the slave showed. He rushed directly at the overseer. Ryder raised the whip hand, not being able to come at Rufus with his fists. The whip descended one time, landing against the charging slave's right shoulder.

Rufus was maddened. He reached out a fist and punched the inactive arm of the hand that Ryder had hurt a while ago. Ryder, against his will, let out a near-scream.

Rufus laughed then, drawing up both hands to the overseer's throat. He gripped it tautly. Ryder threw the useless whip out of his hand, letting it fall in the

109

direction of a dark corner. With his good hand he did his best to pry the maddened black man off him. It did no good. He brought up a knee, but Rufus had stepped to one side and Ryder couldn't turn.

The overseer started to gasp. His breath came with difficulty. His face was becoming light red, then dark. He opened his mouth to get all the air that he could. The energy was drained out of him except for his good hand flailing madly in the air. The hand touched Rufus, but there wasn't enough strength in it to do any harm. A sound passed from his lips like the last gasp of a hog.

With the fight over, Rufus suddenly grinned and began slowly moving the overseer's head and neck back and forth. At the same time he sing-songed, *"Rock-a-bye, baby, on the tree top . . ."*

Grace Parker, who had been rigid for the last few minutes, let out a small breath and took a deep one as if to do it for her overseer. Sam, who had been watching the strangulation, heard the inhaling and looked at the beautiful woman who was afraid.

He called out to Rufus, "Kill him good, boy, kill him real good."

Then he moved closer to the white girl.

"When the bough breaks . . ."

Ryder was coughing and gasping. Blood pounded in Rufus' ears. He had killed four men in his time, but the others had all been slaves and he'd never before had the feeling that a white girl was watching and felt sure that everything he did was vital to the rest of her life.

Behind Rufus there was some noise, but he supposed that Sam was up to something and didn't pay any attention.

". . . the cradle will fall."

On the last word, Rufus confidently took a step back. There was no sign of life in Ryder. He fell face down to the floor, raising a cloud of dust around his body.

110

Rufus was smiling again. "Now that I worked up a little sweat, Grace, gal, I can . . ."

He stopped himself. His eyes cleared and he realized what had been happening in the last few moments. Sam, his friend, was nursing a welt on the right cheek, a fresh welt that was oozing bright red blood. At Grace Parker's side, dog whip in one of two good hands, stood Sebastian.

"Don't come any closer," he warned. "You saw what your friend got and I don't care if a white person's property is blind forever and can't work again. I was aiming for the eyes."

Rufus asked contemptuously, "You think I'm going to let a nigger boy stop me?"

"If you want this whip across the eyes you will. I'm not going to miss two times in a row."

Rufus asked quietly, "Why don't we fight even, with fists?"

"Because your friend will try to do Miss Grace some harm while we're fighting."

"If I tell him to do nothing, he won't do a thing."

"I've got no reason in the world to believe you, and I wouldn't put Miss Grace in danger."

" 'Miss Grace'." Rufus whirled and spat directly in the white girl's face. "Miss Bitch, Miss Whore, you mean! I don't want to hear no more of that 'Miss' Grace coming out of a black boy's mouth not one more time."

The noise above them was becoming almost bearable, and everybody in the cellar could hear the stairs creaking softly under bare feet. Sebastian glanced at Grace Parker encouragingly as if to say that he could handle anybody else who came into this room as well as he was handling these two blacks. He wondered if it was true.

"You like her, don't you?" Rufus asked, as if he was surprised. "She's a good piece for you, isn't that it? Does she do what you want, Sebastian? Does she

111

take it in the mouth? In the ass? What about the nose? What about the armpits?"

Grace Parker's composure wasn't cracked by his talk, although Rufus darted glances at her to see if she was affected.

"Did you ever try it between the titties?" he asked Sebastian. "You pop the tool between 'em and let go and see if she don't open her legs by habit and then open her m—"

Grace was looking out the door, having heard the steps of bare feet and wondering who would be here next and what would happen then. She had always tried to deal with her slaves in a decent and honorable way, but she had always felt that she was sitting on top of a bubbling cauldron. She may have been frightened for her honor and even her life, but she wasn't surprised.

From the doorway Orchid called out, "Sebastian! Thank the Lord you're alive!"

Sebastian would have given anything to take her in his arms, but he spared her only a glance and then said, "Don't come any closer, Orchid."

Orchid looked hurt, but didn't move. Rufus suddenly cocked his head in Sam's direction. Sam, still nursing the cheek welt, hurried to the door and closed it and stood in front of it.

Sebastian sensed danger of a new kind, but he didn't know what form it was going to take. Above all, he could not stand the sight of a relaxed and smiling Rufus.

"I'll make you an offer, Sebastian, and a pretty good one. I mean to celebrate being free by having a gal before too long. Now I admit I'd like to play some games with the white bitch, but I'll settle for Orchid. I've always liked her and you might say I'm jealous on account of your taking her away."

Sebastian understood the danger then. The desire to do murder rose to his brain, but it had to be controlled.

112

"Now, Sebastian, you can't protect both of these here gals and you know it. Sam is so close to Orchid that all he's got to do is move half an inch and he' practically on top of her."

Sebastian's eyes never left those of Rufus. Wouldn't the eyes tell him when danger became nerve-pinchingly acute?

"So I'll do this much, Sebastian," Rufus said. "I'll take the one gal you don't want. Take your pick and do it now, boy. Which one of these gals are you going to throw away? Well, Sebastian? There's no time to think about it."

Sebastian was still. Orchid suddenly let out a bitter sob.

Chapter Nine

On the upper floors of Rootstock, the destruction continued. Every dish had been broken, every bedspring smashed. The walls had been stained by urine and so had some of the floors. Cracked lanterns had been thrown at ceilings in order to scar them.

"We're free!" a slave called Telemachus suddenly shouted. "Every one of us is free!"

A slave named Dromio threw an empty bottle of cooking sherry. It hit Telemachus on the mouth, then broke. Telemachus screamed in pain, but the slaves who didn't know what had happened were sure that he was in an ecstasy of happiness.

A slave named Annabelle started to throw a bottle out of a window. There was no noise of breaking glass, though. Annabelle tried to find out why not and decided that that particular window was broken a long time ago. But she looked out the space where it was and her body became stiff and she stayed there and stared.

The posse was ready by half-past six. A dozen more men had been recruited in town, all of them willing to go out to Rootstock and put down the Negro insurrection.

Eli Crosby looked at them with a sour pleasure. Most of the men had been drinking, but not one of them was drunk. Every man of them could handle the pistol that the town constable had given out.

"Nigger hell is right," he said to himself, and then added more loudly and self-consciously, "but we only shoot if we have to."

The constable, saddling up his horse nearby, said grimly, "From the way you tell it, Mr. Crosby, we sure will have to."

Rufus grinned and said, "Come on, boy, you tell me who you want me to have, which of these two gals, and that's the one I take. Isn't it fair enough? I don't see what I could do to make it more fair, boy."

Sebastian, the whip raised, said nothing and tried to feel nothing. Orchid had put a knuckle between her lips and bit down hard in order to keep from making any other sound, but a keening came from her. She was swaying back and forth as if at prayer. Grace Parker waited, hands at her sides and in front of her hips. Her hands were like claws, poised to strike out at anybody who might come close to her. Her eyes were narrowed to slits and her breath came raggedly.

"What makes you keep so quiet, Sebastian?" Rufus prodded. "Haven't you figured out which of 'em you like the less? You can't have 'em both, you know."

Silence. It never occurred to Rufus, even for the sake of his sadistic little joke, to ask either woman which one wanted him.

He raised his voice. "Can you hear me, Sam?"

"Sure." His close friend, standing near Orchid and in spite of remembered pain, was rubbing both hands together.

"All right." Rufus edged closer to the white girl. "You take the one you're near and I'll take mine on this side of the room, then we switch."

"Great," Sam called. "I figured you might be going soft in the head, offering anything to *him*."

"Not me."

Upstairs, somebody started to shout. Rufus didn't let himself get distracted though. He ducked his head and put one hand up over it with the palm down, hoping to keep any whip-damage as light as possible. Grace drew back. She had shown fear, and that was dangerous in this case. Her breath was coming more heavily.

118

Sebastian brought down the dog whip and cracked it against a point above Rufus' crotch. Rufus screamed in surprise more than pain, stunned at the half-formed notion of what might have happened if the whip had fallen below the point where it landed. He fell back, hands at his crotch in protection.

"Tell the other one to leave my gal alone," Sebastian snapped. "Or next time I aim the whip a little lower."

Rufus snarled, then charged Sebastian. Sebastian drew back, raised the dog whip, and heard it whistle through the air as it landed across Rufus' brow. The slave gasped, his charge halted.

Out of Sebastian's reach, Orchid began to shout. Sebastian could see out of the corner of an eye that Sam had reached her and was holding both her hands in one of his and trying to rip her scanty dress with his free hand. He knew that neither he nor Rufus was going to move an inch. To take a step away from Grace Parker wouldn't keep Rufus from raping her and Orchid, too.

It was Grace Parker who saved Orchid. The white girl suddenly whirled around for the chair under the hangman's rope, raised it and hurled it across the room.

It struck Sam in the head and cracked and creaked as it landed. Sam. swaying dizzily, had to let go of Orchid. The chair was half-broken at his feet. He tripped over it and sprawled on the dust-caked floor.

From above, a woman shouted, "Whites are here! A whole white devil army!"

Sebastian would never know whether Rufus was glad about the interruption. He suddenly turned his back on Sebastian and walked to the door. Sam lay near him. He kicked Sam, who was conscious and murmuring a string of obscenities.

"Stop that and listen," Rufus said urgently. "We

got ourselves some work to do. We give those white devil bastards a surprise like they never forget."

"Okay," Sam murmured.

Rufus looked back of him. "You coming with us, Sebastian? What say?"

"I'll be here."

"In the cellar with the gals," Rufus sneered. "That's about what I figured you to do."

Orchid said stiffly, "I'm going up there to fight."

Sebastian shouted, "Orchid, I forbid you to put your life in danger!"

Orchid answered coolly and quietly, "You just lost the right to forbid me to do anything, Sebastian. You didn't mind just a while ago if I was raped or not. Now I don't mind if you stay down here or not, but I'm going."

She led the other slaves out of the cellar. Rufus glanced behind, sneered and left. The door was open.

Grace asked softly, "Do you want to go upstairs with them, Sebastian?"

"I can't," Sebastian said miserably. "If nobody stays to watch you, those two will come back."

"I'll lock the door."

"They battered it down once, and they could do it again."

"They didn't break the barrier. It raised itself, Sebastian, under pressure. But it's still there."

"After what you did for Orchid, I can't leave you here," Sebastian said. "That's a hard decision to make. I think I ought to be upstairs with my people."

"Instead, you're down here with one person," Grace murmured. "We ought to close the door and lock it as best we can."

He was trudging over there to do it when she stopped him. "Wait! Leave Jack Ryder in front of the door. It'll frighten off any of the others who might come down here, if they see a body."

120

She was probably right. He dragged the dead man out by the armpits. When she put the door bolt in place on the two of them, Sebastian was shaky from close contact with the dead.

Grace Parker suddenly glanced over at the broken chair and said, "You couldn't have been hanged in this room, Sebastian. You'd have had to stand up on that creaking old chair and it wouldn't have held you for a second."

He had been shaking when she started to talk, and now he suddenly let out a gasp. He sat down so that his back was against the wall, shading his eyes with a hand.

All he wanted was to sit for a few minutes and listen to himself breathing and know that he was alive. He had gone through too much, had seen and knew too many things. The world was a death-trap where everything was soaked in blood. The living could die in moments, the dead found no rest. There would be more killings at Rootstock before long. There might be hangings afterward. It was too much knowledge to have gained at one time, too much for him to take in after only a few days.

And softly, above his head, Grace Parker murmured, "You know, Sebastian, I've just had an idea that I think you'll find is pretty interesting."

Orchid reached the first floor before Rufus did. She gazed at the shambles, not believing her eyes. Many of the slaves had passed out drunk. Somebody else was drunkenly moaning a hymn.

"Careful," Alfred said. The house slave had been looking for her. He had spent most of his working life trying to keep the main house neat and clean, but in the shambles he was looking only at her.

"Are you all right?" he demanded.

"Yes. And you?"

"So far." He said, "Maybe we can leave by the back."

"I don't want to leave."

"Stay, and there's sure to be trouble."

"I'll stay."

"In that case, I suppose I will, too."

Rufus had come up the stairs, hurrying. Annabelle, one of the older women, turned to him.

"I threw a bottle out there," she said, pointing to the window, "and didn't hear no crash so I went over to see why not and I seen the whites coming. The window had got busted before."

Rufus checked for himself that a number of whites on horses were moving toward the main house at Rootstock. He turned to Sam.

"You've got to help," he said.

"I'm not too dizzy now," Sam said.

"Okay. I'm going to put one boy in front of every window and I'm going to have him pull up enough of those things," he gestured at the furniture, "so they can hide behind 'em and look out."

"Not too many of the boys are in good shape from what I see."

"We'll use gals when we have to, but I want every window covered. You and me can take them two over there for ourselves. Now let's get busy rousting the others."

Rufus' experience as the best slave driver at Rootstock was useful to him now as the barricades were set up while the white devil bastards came closer. He had never worked more quickly in his life and never been rougher on slaves. He wished he could use Sebastian at one of the windows; Lord knew he hated Sebastian, but the boy was stone cold sober and not a bad fighter when he put himself to work at it.

One of the boys was carrying what looked like a heavy case with glass at one side. Rufus said to him,

122

"Put that stuff down. There's no time to fool around now."

"Will not," the boy said. His name was Hosea, and he had a wide gap-toothed grin. "Look at all them rocks."

Rufus started to glance down, but his gaze rested on them longer than he had expected. There were more stones than he could count, each in a slot of its own. Some of them looked as if they weighed a lot. Rufus remembered having heard that Miss Grace's daddy used to pick up different shaped stones around the plantation and tuck them away.

"All right, Hosey," Rufus said. "You did good. Now give me three of them and pass out the others so we can all use them when we have to."

But Hosea looked mulish. "I want 'em for myself."

"You can take 'em with you down the river when the white devil bastards sell you."

"They won't!"

"Sure they will if you don't take care of yourself now and use everything you can. Now give me that!"

He pulled the box away from Hosea and told each fighter to take three of the rocks. There weren't enough to go around.

"The rest of you can use anything you find that can be thrown." Rufus said. "Throwing is all we've got, and don't you forget that."

There was some muttering, but nobody wanted to challenge Rufus on any ground.

"Now get to your places, all of you," he said. "Here's where we nail them white devil bastards and get ourselves evened up for everything—do you hear? For everything."

The men shouted and cheered like those old-time Hebrew slaves must have done, and then moved to their places. A number of gals moved among them,

123

chuckling as if this was a holiday; soon enough they would know that it wasn't.

Watching them, Rufus decided that no matter what might happen in the time that was to follow, he would never be taken alive. And before he died he was going to take as many white bastards as possible to hell with him.

Chapter Ten

The posse had stopped about fifty feet from the front of the main house. The constable, expecting that he would be the leader said quietly:

"We'll surround the house."

A slaveowner named Preston Barrett laughed scornfully. "Surround a house to get some niggers out? You're a fool."

Press Barrett was a hard-featured man, the veteran of many a drinking bout. He raised cotton, but also had some interests in a Tremont bank and a showboat steamer. His great-grandfather had been a slaver, bringing blacks over to the United States from Africa. Old Hubert Barrett finally quit his career of blackbirding and bought himself some land and started to grow cotton. He was considered a hard master and he died one night in a slave uprising.

Hubert's son, Dover, rebuilt the plantation from the ground up, added to the land and expanded his holdings. He had shown considerable interest in charities, such as helping the poor and the starving. He had put up many a building in Tremont, many which still kept his name. He had been a good man to strangers. But Dover treated his slaves pretty badly. He had died in bed, which a good many of the colored would have sworn wasn't going to happen.

Preston's father, Ned Barrett, had been considered a kind master. Some of the slaves were genuinely sorry when he passed away, leaving everything to his son. All the same, there had been a wild party in the slave quarters on the night of Master Ned's funeral.

Preston Barrett got married at nineteen, but often went to Miss Clara's place in Tremont. He was devoted to his four kids but could thrash them without mercy when he felt he had to. He was a law-abiding man, but had killed three men with a sword and two with a gun. He drank like a fish, but didn't hold his liquor well. He mixed his drinks. When people talked about Press Barrett, they said that he was hard to figure out.

Barrett shook his head vigorously. "I'll roust out those niggers, constable. I've been among niggers my whole life. If a man looks determined, they won't fight him."

"They hate you for the color of your skin," the constable pointed out. "They hate whites."

"I've got a pistol, constable. Get out of my way."

The constable drew back, watching a man destroy himself.

Preston Barrett moved confidently, pistol holstered at his side. He saw the smashed windows barricaded by broken furniture and beady hate-filled eyes that peered out from the barricades. When he was ten feet from the front of the main house, he threw his head back and raised his voice.

"Come out of there," he called in his baritone. "If you don't do no more harm to the house, you won't be hurt for what you done. That's a promise. I know your owner will stand behind it."

Silence. Probably they were too scared to move.

"If you don't start coming out," Preston Barrett said, "I'll be coming in. And I've got me a gun."

The rock was thrown from one of the windows. It hit Preston Barrett flush on the ruddy neck, choking off his breath. He reached for the pistol and had fired three shots in the general direction of the main house before he plunged forward.

From the house a door swiftly opened and a black man hurried out. He moved in a gingerly fashion over to Preston Barrett, circling him.

He looked at the welt on Barrett's neck and nodded in satisfaction that the rock had certainly knocked out the plantation owner. Deftly, he pulled

128

the gun out of Barrett's hand. As he ran directly back toward the door, three shots were sounded by the whites. The slave suddenly tripped and fell, blood oozing from a hole at the back of his head. Just as he fell he managed to throw the gun away from himself toward the opened door. A hand reached out and pulled it inside.

The constable cursed. "Our own bullets finished Press Barrett off, but we damn well have to go in there now. Three men to the front and back and two men to the—"

"Let's go in together," said flat-faced Luke Heather, who owned Downycraft. "It gives us a good chance to yell as if there were hundreds of us. That'll scare 'em good and we ought to run into no trouble whatever."

"You're probably right, Mr. Heather," the constable said quickly, falling in with that influential man's ideas.

One of the volunteers mounted a horse, causing the constable to forget his tact for a moment. "Are you losing your courage so soon?"

The volunteer said, "I wouldn't charge into no coons on foot, friend. I'm taking the horse."

The constable decided that never again would he get a posse together that had anyone other than lawmen on it. These damn fools wanting to do everything their own way would drive him out of his mind.

The pistol had been pulled in by Sam. He snapped the door shut and barricaded it with a chunk of broken furniture.

Rufus, halfway across the shattered room, called out, "Where's Hosey?"

"Dead out there."

"Damn! We could 'a used every boy we got."

Sam had pushed the pistol hurriedly into a pock-

129

et, but when he turned around to admit that Rufus was telling the truth, the pocket-bulge showed itself.

"What have you got there?" Rufus demanded.

"Just a little keepsake."

"You damn fool, throw it away. You'll need all the heft you can get out of the way when the fur starts flying."

"Okay," Sam said agreeably, turning back to the door. He even let Rufus see him put a hand into the pocket so that Rufus would take it for granted Sam had followed orders. Just as he expected, Rufus soon turned around to yell something at somebody else. Sam drew a deep breath and felt lucky at knowing that any white devil bastard coming over to him was going to get something that wouldn't be forgotten. Sam had no intention of dropping the gun or handing it over. He had put his life on the line for that pistol and he was going to hold on to it.

He didn't expect Rufus coming over to him so soon. "I think you're the only one I can be sure will keep an eye out," he said. "Are you still carrying that lump of junk on you after what I said? Hand it over here."

And he reached for it.

Sam drew back, shouting, "It's mine, Rufus, and you keep away if you know what's good for you."

Rufus looked mean. "Is that the gun, Sam? The gun that Hosey gave his life to get for all of us? Are you taking it for yourself?"

Sam knew he shouldn't admit it was the pistol, but he couldn't help trying to win the argument. "Better me for myself than you for yourself."

Rufus' hand snaked out, smacking Sam across his right cheek. "You damn fool, hand me that pistol and do it right now! I don't have to stand for this from you or anybody else."

Sam held one hand over the pistol pocket. He wasn't able to protect himself as well as he might have done otherwise. Rufus flicked a fist almost

130

contemptuously into his middle, doubling him up and forcing him to cover his stomach with both hands. That was when Rufus reached into the bulging pocket.

He tore part of the pocket but didn't get the pistol. Sam had reeled so as to put himself out of Rufus' reach. Rufus kept after him, though, and Sam finally drew the pistol and pointed it at Rufus' chest.

"Get away from me or I give you something you don't forget. Get away from me!"

"All right," Rufus said too quickly. "You win. There's nothing I can do against that thing, is there?"

He shrugged and turned away, but then he whirled and lunged back. The move caught Sam off-guard. He called out and his face grew tense and sweaty. Rufus knocked him down with a fist into the point of his chin. Sam fell, then Rufus tried to kick the pistol out of one hand. Sam raised the pistol, but Rufus simply stomped down on that hand with all his strength.

Sam let out a scream of agony and almost automatically pulled up the other hand to punch hard at Rufus. Rufus balanced his weight to stomp on that other one as well. As Sam dropped the pistol and Rufus bent over for it, bones crunched under his feet. Sam was cursing and crying at the same time.

Rufus picked up the pistol, the first one that he had ever seen, then stepped to one side. He had stood on Sam's hands longer than necessary.

Over Sam's moans, Rufus said, "You're lucky I don't put a hole in you for not doing what I told you."

He didn't have any idea that the little dingus on the right was a safety catch meant to keep the gun from firing unless it was pushed. He pulled the trigger, but it was fast in place and nothing at all hap-

131

pened. He realized that Sam had tried to fire the thing, too, and hadn't known the way to do it.

Damn it, the gun was no good! It had been spoiled after that business outside.

"I'll keep this," he said, dropping it into his own pocket. "I've got a better aim than any of you."

It wasn't going to do any harm to let the others feel sure that somebody on their side carried a pistol, too. Over Sam's groans, Rufus turned to talk to somebody else.

There was a shouting on the outside and Orchid whirled around with narrowed eyes.

"A whole swarm of whites are coming," she called.

Alfred, at her side, added, "It's hard to see, but I'm pretty sure they've got guns."

A slave called out, "We better run!"

"That's what they want us to do," Rufus said through gritted teeth. "We let no whites tell us what to do no more. What we do instead is stay and fight."

Grace Parker said softly, "We're alone and the door is locked. There's still some time for us."

Sebastian, who had been walking moodily, turned to her. "Are you crazy? Here? At a time like this?"

Grace Parker laughed throatily. "Any time is good, Sebastian. Besides, who knows if either of us will ever get a chance to do it again with anybody?"

As he watched, trying to take his eyes away, Grace Parker began to slip out of her dress.

Four of the whites were on horses. The others walked. The walkers carried pistols at their sides, raising them as if to take aim at the darkness itself.

Eli Crosby suddenly gave the urgent whisper:

"*Now,* men, all of you!"

They started yelling at the tops of their lungs as they ran. Horse hoofbeats gave the impression that

132

any number of men were in the charge. Crosby, running with the others, felt himself deafened by the noise.

As the men came closer, a rock was hurled out of the darkness. It struck one of the horses. The rider fell to the ground, shooting his pistol as he dropped.

In the main house, somebody groaned.

The others responded automatically, it seemed, swerving to see how badly the horse was hurt. There was some muttering among slaves inside the house.

The constable looked startled, not being used to anything like this. Crime in Tremont or near it was usually a small matter that didn't mean arresting anybody except a drunk. It never had anything to do with gunplay.

Luke Heather, who owned Downycraft, was telling the limping rider to shoot quickly and aim the pistol toward the building. The marauding slaves would be sure another shot was being fired at them. The rider was arguing that the horse might be saved.

"We've got no time now," Luke Heather said, while a few other men made sympathetic sounds. "It has to be done right away or not at all."

Crosby, dazed with fury, guessed that the men were about fifty feet from the house. His tongue licked his lips as the men wasted valuable time. He could hear birds scolding each other shrilly. He could *feel* the earth churning under his boots.

He nodded to himself decisively, a picture of Grace Parker in bad trouble rising to his mind along with the conviction that he himself would be responsible for it. Swiftly, he detached himself from the others. They prodded horseflesh and he began to hurry around to the side of the main house. His pistol was in hand. He had never felt so alert. In a few minutes Eli Crosby would have settled this whole business.

"Eli," somebody called urgently, "Eli . . . oh,

133

damn it, now the *other* horses are acting up! What the hell can we do?"

Eli Crosby didn't care. He knew what he was going to do, and he knew how and why. Uncertainties had left him as he moved ahead, pistol extended.

Rufus said to Sam, "Go down to the cellar and bring that white bitch up here."

He had said it to Sam because his friend wouldn't give him any back talk.

Sam, holding out his hands, said, "These are hurting so much now I can't think about nothing else."

"Go down there or I stomp on 'em again."

Sam left. Rufus never seemed to remember what he had done a little while ago. Rufus figured everything was the way he thought it was. Sam shrugged irritably, moving quickly as he could.

Rufus checked that the others were as ready for trouble as he was. One of the gals wasn't at her place, though. He hurried forward, angry, and saw that she was lying on the floor and that Orchid was watching Alfred try to soothe her.

"There's nothing wrong," Rufus said fiercely.

Alfred eased the gal's head down to the floor as Rufus watched in the near-darkness.

"She's dead now," he said. "That first shot did for her."

Orchid said softly, "Alfred, you couldn't have done more than you did to help. You're a good man, Alfred."

Rufus snapped, "Now you've done everything you can, so throw the body out the window."

Alfred said, "You'll have to do it yourself."

"No guts? You're a good man all right, Alfred, except when there's trouble." Rufus bent down and threw the body outside. There was another shot nearby and they all heard a noise like the one that a horse would make.

134

When Sam got back to the big room he was alone.

"Where's the white devil?" Rufus asked furiously.

Sam said. "His body is in front of the cellar door, and I tripped over it."

"I didn't ask you about Jack Ryder," Rufus said while a dozen slaves in earshot murmured superstitiously. "I meant the white devil bitch. Why didn't you bring her up here like you were told?"

Sam held up his hands. "I couldn't open the door. I've got no power in these, and I didn't want to yell when I couldn't back up anything I might say."

Rufus snarled. "I'll take care of it myself, then. If something more should happen up here, I'll come running. Sam, you watch to make sure that nobody goes asleep on the job or starts to fun around."

One of the slaves muttered, "With Mister Jack as the overseer, at least I could get me some sleep when it was nighttime."

Rufus hurried down the stairs. He had been warned about the overseer's body, but in the darkness he nearly tripped on it himself.

He kicked at the door with his feet and hit it with his hands. "Hurry up and let me inside, you two! Hurry up or I kill the both of you like I did that white one. Hurry up!"

There was an edge of hysteria in his voice, of desperation and fanaticism. Sebastian, on the the other side of the door, was going to remember it later on.

Sebastian and Grace had heard Sam trip over the dead body. Sebastian glanced up as far as he could see in near-darkness.

"I'm going up there," he said, reaching for the dog whip. "For both our sakes, you'd better come with me."

"I don't suppose there'll be much of a choice if you're up there," she said carefully. "You're the only protection I've got, Sebastian." She had swiftly taken both hands away from her dress.

135

He was near the door when the kicking and pounding started. Carefully, he opened it. There was a sliver of light from the direction of the stairs. He could see Sam, and stepped back.

"I want the white devil bitch upstairs," Sam said.

"We'll both go." Sebastian reached for the dog-whip.

He helped her to keep from tripping over Jack Ryder's body. Sam, watching, laughed.

"No nigger goes around helping white gals unless he gets something out of it," Sam said. "You've been getting some good white meat there."

A lantern had been kicked against one wall of the upper level, and wooden matches thrown against another. Sebastian lit the lantern, causing most slaves to call out at what seemed like harsh lighting after so much darkness.

She was gasping at sight of the damage she could make out. To her nose, the smells in this room were unbearable.

Sebastian called out, "Orchid? Orchid, are you here?"

There was no answer, but the silence around him was charged. He knew that Orchid was in the room. He suddenly saw Orchid turn from one of the windows and walk toward him. Her lips were tautly pursed and he waited for her to talk. But she didn't say a word. She drew her head back and spat in his face.

Rufus, who had been pacing the room, looked satisfied as he turned. "The white devil bitch is here. Okay. Now I can go ahead."

"What do you mean, 'I can go ahead?' " Sam asked uneasily. "I swear I think you've gone—" Sam swallowed at the menacing look in Rufus' eyes. "No, wait, wait. I'm sorry I said that."

Rufus wasn't soothed, but he did look away. "Now it's time," he said softly. "Now it's the time, all right. *It's the time!*"

136

Sebastian didn't think that he'd ever forget the wild look in Rufus' darting, staring, wide eyes. He shivered and wished he knew why he should be so uneasy, so damned extra-special uneasy.

Eli Crosby couldn't know that he reached the side of the house at a time when a lantern was going on in one of the rooms. The slaves at the windows felt blinded.

He climbed in through a window, pushing furniture to one side as he moved. It was dark, but the floor was cluttered. The smell in the house was dreadful. The house would probably have to be smashed down to the ground and built up all over again from the foundation.

He hadn't realized how dark it would be. Although he was listening to murmurs all around him, he didn't know how many slaves were in this room or if any were here. Nor did he have any notion where he was.

Luckily, he didn't have to grope. A thread of light could be seen under the door leading to the next room. He was able to stand still, confident that somebody was in the next room. As soon as that door opened he would shoot.

Meanwhile, he told himself not to breathe too loudly and not to move. The floor would creak when his weight was changed in balance. A time passed in which nothing happened. He told himself he might as well have stayed outdoors and slept. He hadn't counted on the darkness and the clutter and the miserable smell.

He raised his pistol when the door opened and then he fired.

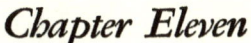

Chapter Eleven

Sebastian turned away from Orchid, speaking to Grace, "Let's move away from here."

Grace Parker tucked a tendril of blonde hair back into place and said to Orchid, "You're making a mistake. Sebastian is a good man."

Orchid wouldn't have talked to Sebastian, but she did talk to Grace. "I'm sorry, Miss. I'm sorry for so much."

Grace nodded and walked away softly, almost floating in her movements. She thought nothing of going in first, probably because it never occurred to her that there was any danger in the house that Sebastian couldn't attend to.

And so she opened the door. Rufus yelled to call her back. There was a shout of triumph from somewhere in the next room. The pistol shot was unbearably loud.

Sebastian's first move was instinctive. He flicked the whip, sending the lantern out of Grace Parker's suddenly nerveless fingers. The lantern fell to the floor, most of its glass shards cracking into smaller shards. The light hadn't gone out, though, as Sebastian had hoped. He could see the hard, white, sweat-streaked face of Eli Crosby in the next room. Crosby could see him as well. There was a hard gleam in the white man's eyes, a gleam of malice to be caught forever in Sebastian's mind. The room stank of cordite on top of the other smells.

It was impossible to flick the pistol out of Crosby's hand as it was raised toward Sebastian. There was too much space between them.

It was Grace who saved him for the moment, perhaps without meaning to, but possibly on purpose. She had been swaying back and forth, badly wounded. Now she fell, her body descending on the exposed lantern flame. For a moment the room was again smothered by darkness. Sebastian ducked and swerved out of the path of danger even as the pistol exploded one more time.

As he moved, safe for the moment, he knew that the odor of burning human flesh had been added to the others in the suffocating room. Grace Parker's body was on fire.

Just before the pistol shot sounded, Rufus had been talking quietly to Sam.

"Nobody's going to give up in this fight!" Rufus said. "Nobody whatever!"

And Sam, still skeptical, asked, "What made you decide that, Rufus?"

"Do you remember that story about them old-time Hebrews?" Rufus asked cunningly. "They wouldn't go back to slavery so they killed each other."

Sam's first impulse was to laugh. "You're not saying that you expect us all to go around killing each other?"

Rufus stood silently, his eyes closed, his lips moving, his hands twitching. His body swayed lightly. A moment passed before Sam realized that the big bald man's head was moving up and down slowly.

Staring at him, Sam felt a touch of fear against his neck, and the fear wasn't so close to him on account of anybody outside this house.

"We'll all be damn fools if we don't," he said. "Once it looks hopeless, that's what we have to do."

"Rufus, you've really gone stark staring cra—"

"Don't say that word," Rufus put in quickly. "For your sake and mine, Sam, don't say it."

The shot interrupted each man. Rufus jumped and whirled around, then raced for the door. He reached the next room as a sheet of flame started up and around the white girl's body. There was a white man with a pistol and Sebastian with a dog whip. As Rufus and Sam appeared, Eli Crosby's pistol wavered. That was long enough for Sebastian to take two swift steps forward and raise the whip to try and flick the pistol out of Crosby's hand.

He had moved to Crosby's right so as not to be in direct range of the deadly muzzle, and in the time it took him Crosby fired again and then again.

Sam let out a gasp, having been spun halfway around by the bullets at impact, and flame singed his body as he fell.

The whip descended with a snap and the pistol skidded out of Eli Crosby's pain-wracked hand.

Rufus didn't turn to look at his dead friend, nor pay any attention to the fire that might devour everybody in the house. Instead, hands outstretched, he started toward Eli Crosby. The white slaveowner tried to face down the slave, but one look at his eyes and he decided to run instead.

Sebastian picked up the pistol, then tucked it into a pocket; there would certainly be some use for it later on. Then he turned back to the door and shouted:

"Fire here! Fire! Come and help me put it out, three of you. Hurry!"

Other slaves hurried into the room. As flames mounted the walls, Rufus' angry black hands found Eli Crosby's thick neck.

The horses had stopped screaming and running, crashing into each other and drawing back with whinnies of terror.

Luke Heather said, "We go in now, boys."

"But some of the animals could start going crazy again," the constable protested weakly, exhausted from his efforts at trying to gentle the animals.

"The hell with that," Luke Heather shouted. "There are two people in that damn house!"

Rufus let Eli Crosby's body fall to the floor. The slaves behind him were trying to stamp out the fire,

143

but it wasn't easy. It seemed to Rufus that the flames were rising. He stumbled out of that room to where slaves were starting to run to the back door and what they hoped would be safety and freedom.

"Get back to your places, all of you," Rufus thundered. "There is nothing to be afraid of. I'm telling you this—Rufus."

A woman shouted, "Nobody can stay here for long."

"If you want to stay, Sarah, that's what you do. You're nobody's slave now. You don't belong to anybody except you yourself, thanks to old Rufus."

"May the Lawd be good to you, Rufus, but—"

"Well, you can be good to me later on, honey."

There was a roar of laughter and the girl said:

"If it wasn't so hot, I wouldn't mind getting me something to eat."

Rufus chuckled. "I can give you that, too, honey."

The laughter swelled, but nobody moved. Rufus turned to a man and asked him to come into the next room. When Rufus was satisfied that the others had drifted back to their barricaded windows, he turned to the man who had waited for him and said:

"Spart, nobody's coming out of this alive."

The slave named Spartacus, a small fellow, nodded. "Thanks for telling me, Rufe. I'll get away now."

"Nobody can get away," Rufus growled. "We push ourselves to the wall, like them ancient Hebrews. We kill each other, but we don't get sold down the river."

"That's crazy!"

Rufus didn't wait any longer. His hands knew the way to a human being's neck and knew what to do when they got there. A few gurgles, a desperate attempt to kick out and that was the end of it. Rufus pushed the body away into a corner. As he started to the door, it opened on Alfred and Orchid. He

144

knew Alfred's voice without being able to see him at the moment, and it stood to reason that nobody would be with the ex-house slave but Orchid. She hung on his arm; her eyes shone; she looked prayerfully happy.

"Rufus, is that you?" Alfred asked politely.

"What about it?"

"Me and Orchid over here, we just now decided to get married. I don't suppose we'll be able to now, but we wanted everybody to know."

"Get married?" Rufus' wits were so scattered that it took a pause before he could remind himself what they must be talking about. "Sure, get married. I seen the preacher do that a lot of times."

"And if we come out of this, you'll be my best man," Alfred said. "For letting us have the chance to get together and for letting us hold our heads up for a while, at least."

"Why, that's good of you, Alfred, and I'm honored." Rufus grinned. "But you don't have to wait for the preacher. I'll marry you right now, just like the preacher. I can marry you better than the preacher, believe me."

"It wouldn't be the same."

"Watch and see. Now you two hold each other's hands. Got 'em? Okay. In the sight of the Lord God I say that these two people love each other and will do that forever as long as they live. For that reason they should die as man and wife. From now on they are husband and wife. Amen to that."

"That's not the regular form," Alfred said quietly. "But maybe it's better than the regular form. Maybe it comes more from the heart than when a preacher says it."

Rufus asked in a different tone of voice, "Have you still got each other's hands? Okay, now kiss on the lips."

Dimly, he saw the two heads come closer.

That was when Rufus drew up his hands. Alfred

died quickly. Orchid's scream became a gurgle. Then she, too, was dead.

Sebastian had seen that the fire couldn't be put out. The slaves fell back, reeling and gasping at the effort. It surprised Sebastian, drawing back from the searing flame, that his mind was able to work at all.

He realized that Orchid was in Alfred's care now and that he couldn't survive unless he got away from Rootstock. Rufus may have thought he was putting up a good fight, but the fight was doomed. Sebastian's job was to get away.

He looked out the window and saw white men headed toward the main house, pistols at the ready. Swiftly, he turned and, calling out a warning, ran to the next room. He tripped over something in his hurry, realized it had once been warm and human and female . . . but he kept running.

Rufus, having made out his presence, shouted, "Sebastian, come over here."

"There's no way I can help you," Sebastian said. "Whites are coming and they've got pistols."

"*I've* got a pistol," Rufus said, not admitting that he didn't know how to use it. "We can both stand 'em off."

"No, we're lost if we stay."

"You've got a pistol of your own and the whip as well. You'll be all right. If we stay together, we can't lose."

Sebastian hesitated, finding Rufus oddly persuasive. He couldn't help feeling that after the running he had done the notion of two men with guns standing off a horde of whites was theatrical enough to keep him in place.

Rufus was coming closer. The steps were soft, but determined. Rufus' hands were raised, the fingers stretched, almost as if he was going to give some benediction.

146

The nearest door opened on another slave, who drawled out, "What did you want, Rufus?"

"Who is that? Deacon? C'mon in, Deac. You and me and Sebastian over here—the three of us are going to let them whites have themselves something to remember. Sebastian, give Deacon your whip. No, give it to me and I'll pass it over to him."

Sebastian hadn't moved. Every screaming nerve in his body warned him against letting the weapon out of his hand.

"I'm waiting," Rufus said patiently, a hand outstretched with the palm up.

Sebastian was about to pass the whip when Deacon suddenly shouted:

"Who's this on the floor?"

Rufus snapped, "Shut up, Deac!"

There was the sound of something being moved along the floor. Sebastian, looking to his right, saw Deacon pushing a body closer to the window. "This is Alfred over here, and he's dead."

"Everybody dies sometime," Rufus said quickly. "That's enough out of you."

"Alfred's had his neck pushed in. Who did that, Rufus?"

"I told you to shut up, Deacon!" Rufus thundered.

"And that gal over there—it would have to be Orchid, wouldn't it? What happened to them, Rufus? Rufus, what are you —?"

There was a high-pitched gurgle from Deacon. Seconds after it ended, a body struck the floor. Sebastian, rooted to the spot, had never dreamed that it could take such a short time to kill another human being with the hands. He realized, too, that he had nearly stepped on Orchid's dead body a while ago. Rufus had killed her along with Alfred.

He wondered why he wasn't shocked and sickened. Then he realized that he had become too hardened to death and violence to feel anything ex-

147

cept a queasy gratitude that he for one was still alive.

"Why?" he asked quietly as Rufus straightened. "Why are you killing your own?"

"Why? You should know better than anybody else."

"Me?"

"You're the one who talked about them old-time Hebrews who killed each other instead of going back to slavery. Well, we're as good as they ever were, and I'm going to be the leader of a slave revolution where the blacks kill themselves but won't go back to where they were."

"But you're the one who's killing them," Sebastian blurted out. "They're not killing each other."

"It makes no difference."

Sebastian didn't think that the other man was crazy. Nor was he surprised. He had found out a while ago that he was in a section of the country where life didn't mean much. He had seen so much blood and violence in the last few days that his only instinct was to survive.

"I'll tell you something else, Sebastian," Rufus said, his voice seeming to rise and fill the dark room. "You aren't going out of here without your neck stretched."

Sebastian didn't give away his location by talking any more. He walked backward to the far door. As he moved, he raised the pistol.

"Got you!" Rufus called, and Sebastian guessed that the slurring steps he took had given away his location.

Rufus was moving toward him when he and Sebastian heard the front door crashed in by the attacking whites. The drift of air through the house gave new life to the nearby fire. Flames reached the door from which Sebastian had come in. Rufus was able to see Sebastian perfectly, but there was no longer any time to do anything about it.

148

"It's the fire one way and the whites the other way!" Rufus shouted. "You're going to be a hero man if you like it or not!"

Shots could be heard near the front of the house, shots mixed with the crackle of flame at the rear and the screaming of trapped slaves.

Sebastian hurried to a window and pushed furniture to one side, using his feet when he could, but finding it necessary to put the pistol in his pocket and the whip down on the windowsill.

A slave was running past the sheet of flame into the room. As the slave ran in, eyes bulging and mouth wide with fear, Rufus reached for his neck. There was that horrible gurgle, then the slave fell.

Not looking back, Sebastian put one leg out the window and followed it with the other. The jump to grassy earth below was bigger than he had expected, but he made it without damage.

Chapter Twelve

Rufus walked among the survivors and strangled every one with whom he made contact. He didn't know names or faces. He didn't care. Not one of them was going to be a slave again.

"Oh Lawd, give me strength," he called out, and brought up his hands to a man's neck.

Desperation was giving him strength. He had to take big steps to keep from stepping on anything that wasn't part of the wooden floor, and a ceiling beam missed him by inches.

He no longer knew how many he had killed, but he knew he wanted to kill them. He enjoyed killing them. Never before had he felt so much power. *He* was the slaveowner now, and their lives were in his keeping. He was decreeing death. Oh, he might tell himself he was doing it for a noble reason, but that wasn't true. Dear Lord, how he loved to kill!

He hadn't been watching his steps too carefully as he walked among the dead. A corpse appeared, it seemed, under his foot, and he tripped. He was on one knee. A sound of ripping that he wouldn't have heard before made him look up in time to see part of the ceiling give way in flames.

Unable to get up on time, Rufus raised both fists and cursed the ceiling for coming down on his people. He shouted and tried to get up, but a ceiling beam stunned him. He lay without being able to move. The house crashed. He could hear the groans of slaves trapped in the wreckage. The flames raged around him, trapped like a dog; but he wasn't losing consciousness.

Would he ever die? Did the Lord want him to see all of the destruction?

"No, I'm not sorry!" he cried as loudly as he was able. "It's better to die like this than live like a pig! I'm not sorry!"

Not until the roof fell did Rufus die.

The white men crashed through the door and began their orgy of death.

Luke Heather charged in, pistol firing. A slave fell over, dead. Luke killed another man who was raising a chair. Firelight made eyes glow, made hands look yellowish-green, and helped hide the sounds of screams. A slave whirled on him, pushing a table leg at Luke Heather's head. It missed. Heather fired. The slave reeled, cursed, spat at Luke Heather, fell and died.

Terry Marble, one of the town loafers who had been picked to help the constable and had been hoping to get some loot out of it, hurried inside unwillingly because somebody was back of him. One look at the place and he turned around, waiting for his chance to leave.

His pistol was out, but he hadn't made any plans to use it. He was hoping that he'd be able to sell it when he got away from here. After all, he could sell anything to almost anybody. He would usually sell stolen merchandise and give the buyer some song-and-dance about the struggle for decent employment in a cruel land, as well as the need for dignity in the working man who should never accept charity. His speaking voice was smooth and mellow, as a girlfriend had once told him, adding that it sounded like butter being churned. Terence Oliver Marble had considered that a compliment.

He could imagine the pitch he'd make when it came time to sell the pistol. "It occurs to me," he would say, "that the pistol is an instrument blessed by God in His infinite mercy. It permits us to kill without having to go near the victim or touch him in any way. Any sensitive man would find such a contact repugnant, I feel sure."

A sheet of flame suddenly leaped up to bar his way. Terry Marble reeled, headed for a window.

154

One slave suddenly reached for him and brought both hands up to his throat. Terry felt the life leaving his body. He squirmed, but he had never been too strong. He was dead before his body hit the floor.

The slave who had killed Terry, Marcus, reached for a knife and tried to cut the head off from the back of the neck. It was a brutally messy job and couldn't be done, he realized even before one of the constable's bullets killed him.

Marcus' body lay in front of Luke Heather when that plantation owner ran out of bullets. He threw the thing out the window. He tripped over the dead slave's body and cursed him. The fire was becoming hotter, being fed by air through the shattered windows.

Luke Heather fell to the floor. Somebody stepped on him, but passed over quickly enough. It had been a slave, of course, somebody shouting gibberish and close to hysteria. Luke Heather devoutly hoped he would never see anything like this again as long as he lived. Carefully, he got up.

There was a hand-to-hand fight between Carey Mallon and one of the slaves, Heather saw. Carey was pushing the slave against a fiery wall, but the slave suddenly found a desperate spurt of energy and pushed the white man's head down to his shoulder. Carey started to gurgle. Luke Heather reached that slave in three swift steps. He kicked the slave twice. The slave let go of Carey.

"Got your pistol?" he asked Mallon.

The dazed man pointed to a pocket.

The slave suddenly made a leap for Luke Heather, but the plantation owner stepped back swiftly and took the pistol out of Mallon's pocket. He had heard the slave, distracted, turn around and butt Mallon. The white doubled up and the slave's hands darted for his neck. Mallon had the sense to duck and his body hit the floor. The man stood on him, a foot on his neck. He stood and put pressure on the neck. Mallon gurgled.

Luke Heather put one bullet into the slave but he didn't stop what he was doing.

He put a second bullet into his stomach. The man groaned but wouldn't move from Mallon's body.

Luke Heather's third bullet hit the slave between the eyes. The man tumbled over, dead, beside the body of Carey Mallon.

Luke Heather looked down grimly. Who would have known that Carey would be dead before this night was over? Or Eli Crosby? Or Grace Parker? Or one of the townspeople who had come with them. In the midst of life, as the preacher fellows always said, we are in death.

It was all their fault, Luke Heather told himself as he lurched away. They were the hardest of animals for a slaveowner to work with, the burden of a slaveowner's life. Slavery was no burden to the beast of the field, such as any nigger was. The slaveowner was like a lion tamer who had to give his lions the run of his home area. The ways of the Lord certainly passed all understanding, as the preachers always said.

The constable was shouting, "It's gonna give, the whole house! I'm getting out! We've all killed enough, enough!"

Other white men followed. Luke Heather was the man who stopped to make sure that nobody else in the place would give him any trouble. Then he put Carey Mallon's pistol in a pocket and got out of the house.

The roof gave way at last, just two minutes after he was out of there. Luke Heather liked to tell his friends afterwards that the Lord had sure watched over him on that night.

Sebastian lay flat against the earth. The whip was

156

under him and the gun in his outstretched hand. He had to catch his breath if only for a second.

Behind him, timbers crackled and screams and gunshots could be heard. How long would the house be a living inferno?

And was he going to be safe out here? He decided to inch forward slowly so as not to be seen if any men were waiting outside.

He had to go more quickly, though. Timbers were shattering behind him, dropping in flames to the grass. No man could live and stay near that house of hell.

Sebastian straightened, his pistol ready to be fired. He started to run. A section of the house caved in as he hurried, and some of the furniture from a barricade landed close to him. He tried to zigzag out of danger's way and fell, rolling headlong. He had lost the whip as he rolled down the hill. He was wildly discharging the gun until he knew that there wasn't another bullet left. He opened a hand to let the gun go, but realized he had spread both hands open. The whip was gone as well.

Something wet was on his face. He opened his eyes. The first thing Sebastian saw in the dawn was a pair of hands held tightly over his face. The hands parted, drenching his face in spring water for the second time in half a minute.

He tried to talk, but words came slowly. "I didn't know any of us got through that fire."

Softly at his side a white man's voice said, "You ain't hurt too bad. You'll be all right after a while."

Sebastian drew back at sight of a white man rocking back and forth on his haunches. He supposed that the man wanted to hurry him off someplace into slavery, and almost wished he was back in the burning mansion.

"I won't go," he muttered. "You'll have to carry me."

"You *can* walk," the white man said swiftly. "But

157

I've got my wagon on top of the hill. I came in my wagon because Dick Hooper can't drive for sour apples."

"I don't know what you're talking about and I'm not going anyplace in somebody's wagon."

"In that case, I'll have to persuade you, I suppose," the white man said. He wore a pistol holstered on his right hip, but didn't make a move toward it. He was small, with faded, blond hair that was thinning on top. "I'm with the volunteer fire department and we finally got the fire squashed out. Afterward, well, I wanted to relieve myself so I went over here to do it and I found you."

Sebastian asked carefully, "What are you planning to try and do with me?"

"I suppose you want another master to work for," the white man said. "I'll try and get somebody who won't treat you wrong. What else do you want done?"

"Suppose I want to go up North, instead of getting another slave master?"

"Is that what you want? You'd be surprised how few of your people in chains really want to be their own masters." The white man blinked. "You talk different for a slave. Like you came from the North in the first place."

"I do." Sebastian swallowed. "I was illegally put into slavery when I came South as part of my job."

He knew that there was more money for the white man in not believing him, so that the white man probably wouldn't care about whatever he said.

But the white man, distracted, suddenly put in, "Is that right, now? I lived for a while up at Cincinnati. That's around Ohio way. Do you know it?"

"I think I passed outside it when I was on my way here. I'm not sure." He had to be civil while the white man decided whether he would live or die. "A lot has happened since I left Boston."

"I believe you."

158

The white man stood up. "I'm going to head up for the wagon. If the coast is clear, I'll signal you. What you have to do is get into the back and hide under the straw. You'll be able to breathe all right."

"Hide? Where do you plan to take me?"

"My place first off, so you can get a decent meal and some sleep," the white man said. "Then we'll get you back North. I've got the contacts for doing it. You've heard of the Underground Railroad, I'm sure. Well, I've got some pretty good—ha-ha!—connections."

The man smiled and winked, then headed up the small hill. Sebastian didn't know whether or not to believe a southerner about anything at all, let alone any matter so important to him as this one. The man waved him up. Sebastian would have mulishly refused to go, but the southerner was carrying a gun and could persuade any man who didn't do what he wanted.

Sebastian got to his feet, conscious of pain as the circulation worked its way back into his body. He ran as best he could, his feet stinging with every step. The white man watched him get into the hay wagon and was riding again before Sebastian could get out. The ride was so bumpy and quick, and Sebastian's senses so pain-racked that he couldn't bring himself to get out. Simply looking toward the ground made him dizzy.

"I told you to hide," the white man said when the ride was over. They were in front of a small, neat-looking house at the north end of Tremont. "Lucky we weren't seen. Come on inside."

Sebastian held back. The white man thought it was out of weakness and dizziness that Sebastian wouldn't move. He offered Sebastian a hand. Sebastian shrugged it away and went in under his own steam.

As soon as he was inside he was confronted by a small, energetic woman. She had been cooking, and

159

the smell of greens and chicken was vivid in the nostrils.

"You need something to eat," she said promptly. "I'm getting lunch ready. You don't look like you've had any breakfast. Sit down at the table and I'll rustle something up for you."

"At the table?" Sebastian blinked. "*Your* table?"

"It's the only one we've got," the woman said cheerfully.

He ate like a man in a dream. Then he was led to a small room where he'd be able to sleep for a while. He told himself that he would be safe. With that knowledge he suddenly began to cry in reaction to everything that had happened to him in the last few days. The tears wouldn't stop, it seemed. He cried in part because he missed Orchid and Alfred and even Grace. He cried because he felt guilty at being alive when the others were dead. He cried and felt ashamed of himself, but couldn't stop.

The white man who had saved him came running in. "What in Heaven's sweet name is wrong?"

"Nothing," Sebastian said, but only after he had dried his tears and taken a deep breath. "I haven't done that since I was a baby, but I've seen so much in the last few days that I couldn't help myself. There's nothing wrong now."

"Nothing?" The white man scratched his jaw. "Well, I'm glad there isn't any real reason for the waterfall. If you ever really get upset about something, though, give me and the missus at least three days notice so we can get an ark ready and stock it up with animals the way Noah did. Because when you get all weepy like you just did, why, there's no flood that's in the same class with you."

"I won't do that again." Sebastian smiled weakly. "I won't, I promise. You—you've been very good to me."

The white man looked embarrassed. "Try and get

160

some rest. You've got a week of heavy traveling to get done with."

The white man's face was still flushed with embarrassment when he left Sebastian alone.

Chapter Thirteen

The First Boston Repertory Company was still on its southern tour when Sebastian got back to Boston, and he knew he'd have to get a job to keep him going for a while. He found something on the docks, but only because a white docker took a liking to him. On his first night off the job, the white docker tried to make love to him. Sebastian hit the docker squarely in the body. He didn't bother going back to the dock next morning. The job wouldn't be there any longer.

He had been sharing a room in a cheap boarding house, but on his third night back the colored landlady told him that he wasn't wanted any longer.

"What's wrong?" he demanded. "I'm paying you by the day, like you want."

"You howl around too much at night and the other gentlemen in the room with you can't get their night's sleep."

Sebastian bit his lip. "I ve got to get a place, though. I'll take a private room."

"No, you'd only keep your window open and then the whole neighborhood could listen to the way you roar around."

"I've been getting nightmares lately, and I'm sure you know the reason." He had told her what he had been through. With relatives in the South herself, the landlady had been sympathetic. "I'm sure it'll stop soon."

"I'm sorry about all that, boy, believe me," the landlady said. "But if I keep you inside of a million feet of this house, I lose some of my other gentlemen and I can't afford that. Times isn't what they ought to be."

Sebastian managed to get most of a night's sleep in the park, but he was arrested toward morning for vagrancy. A sympathetic judge in a crowded courtroom heard part of his story and saw that he was carrying enough money with him to have paid for a night's lodging at any colored boarding house in Boston.

"Why don't you go around to the Negro Improvement Association?" the judge suggested. "They'll get you something."

The Negro Improvement, as it was known, was located in a ramshackle building in the south end of the city. A fellow named Teddy Squires, who had a gray-edged mustache, looked doubtful when he heard Sebastian's story.

"Well, I'll let you sleep here, if you want to," he said. "You can sweep up in the morning and dust around to pay for the courtesy."

Sebastian took the offer. The office was always littered with folders which the Negro Improvement gave out. The folders told colored people that they were a different race, rather than just being people of color, and that they ought to call themselves Negroes. They ought to educate their families, and fathers shouldn't leave their wives and kids for other women.

Sebastian, looking at one of the folders, added loudly, "And slavery ought to be wiped out."

Squires, who had just come in for the day's work, chuckled and said, "I'm not really too sure about that."

"For God's sake, why not?"

"Why, it helps establish a Negro identity. Take away mutual fears and grievances to bring Negroes together, and there's really not much reason to stay together or to keep supporting an improvement association."

"So you think that slavery is a good thing because it gives this group more money is that it?"

"It's not a good thing, but we'd have to do plenty of reorganizing without it."

A number of colored people had drifted in while

166

the two of them were talking. He turned to them and told what had happened to him, how he had been shanghaied and had become a tool of white people until he was helped to get away. He saw pity and disgust among the audience, which more people were joining quickly as he talked.

"I have myself been a part of a slave insurrection," he shouted. "And when there was no hope, the slaves imitated the ancient Hebrews by killing each other instead of going back into slavery. Their leader, Rufus, a good and powerful man, gave them inspired leadership for as long as he could . . ."

He knew perfectly well that he was making a hero out of a madman he hated with all his heart and soul. But if it would help this cause he was willing to make Rufus' name immortal. He called Rufus a true friend of his people and a great man, and practically bowed his head when he praised Rufus' memory. He was living a lie and hiding his feelings, hiding his dislike for most of the brutalized slaves, for animal-like people with whom he didn't have anything in common except an accident of birth.

He finished his little speech by saying that a lot of white people in the North and in the South felt the way he did.

Somebody jeered, "If the whites want to free the Southern Negroes it's because they'll make more money out of 'em once they're free."

And somebody else asked, "What about them dockworkers and their outfit? What about that, huh?"

"Those whites are wrong," Sebastian said.

A number of dockworkers, it seemed, had formed a society to stop anti-slavery agitation. Slavery, they said, was a private Southern matter and they didn't want any agitation against friendly states who might declare war and get a lot of people mixed up in it.

"It's like people talking about your wife," one docker had said. *"Slavery is a private matter."*

167

Sebastian stopped. The talk had been going on for half an hour and colored men were running in and out to suggest that other people come inside to hear the talkers.

Teddy Squires, Sebastian's opponent, cleared his throat. Squires wore thick-rimmed glasses and a gold watch chain on his vest and sideburns coming down to his chin. He had a hooked nose and lips like twin plates.

"I sympathize with my young friend's anguish," Squires said, speaking easily and well, "but our slaves are the descendants of slaves and wouldn't be good for much else. If they were set free overnight, friends, what would happen? They would become beggars and the South would be plagued with them. The South would have to give them public assistance of some sort."

"The hell with the South!" somebody called out. "They owe it to our people for keeping 'em in chains!"

"Ah, but the slaves, the ex-slaves, wouldn't all stay in the South. They'd come North, many of them as far as Boston. Many of them would go on public assistance up here and many of them would try and take away the jobs that we've got. And how many of us want to give away our jobs to back up any convictions we may have? After all, how many jobs for colored people do there happen to be in this city?"

Sebastian bit his knuckles, especially because it seemed to him that the audience was murmuring in sympathy with Squires.

"I know that these sentiments aren't popular with colored, but let's be honest. Colored folk may tell the whites one thing about themselves, but among our own we know what colored folk are really like. The ex-slaves who wouldn't take your jobs really would turn into public charges and we know that. Is there somebody here who hasn't been ashamed and disgusted at one time or another by seeing one of

168

our people dead drunk and rolling in the gutter where whites can mock them? Do we need any more of that kind of colored here in Boston?"

There was some applause and surprisingly few jeers. Teddy Squires had played on every unconscious fear in his audience, it seemed. The people may not have liked what Squires told them, but they felt sure there was more than enough truth in it.

In rebuttal, Sebastian spoke swiftly and cuttingly. It wasn't a matter of protecting yourself, but a matter of human decency. He talked again about the insurrection, but didn't feel that his grip on the audience was as tight as usual when he brought up the subject.

Squires, as before, said what many people in the audience were really thinking. "We have heard this story so often that we can't help being a little tired of it by now. There may be some truth in it and some of the incidents may have happened as my young friend says they did—"

Damn him!

"—but they don't have any value in talking about slavery. I don't doubt that slavery has its faults and injustices, but I don't know why we should try to do anything about it and risk what we have won for ourselves in the process."

Sebastian was so angry this time that he grew tongue-tied and had to stop himself half a dozen times in the next few minutes. His fury wasn't helping to hold the audience, and he finally stammered out something about how much freedom would mean to the children of the slaves.

"A child," Squires said, when it was his turn again, "whether it's white or black—or pink or purple, for that matter—needs the influence of a mother and father if it is ever to amount to anything on this Earth. In slave cases, where the child is deserted by both parents and one mother may have had eight children by eight different slaves, there can be no

169

stability whatever. Even here in the North under freedom, we know how many mothers leave their children and how few mothers and fathers live together. And we know the way most of those children grow up and we know what becomes of them. We know because we read in the papers about the crimes they commit and we feel a deep and lasting shame. With the children of slaves we'd know a greater increase in the rates of crime and I feel sure we all realize that."

Sebastian said as carefully as he could that no man was able to be selfish in this problem. Everybody had to pitch in and help. He was so angry it was hard to speak.

Squires said, "To those of us who have been out of work, the whole issue of slavery comes down to self-protection. Slaves are not part of our own lives and their problems don't really concern us. I know that this is a selfish point of view, but it is the truth and we have to admit it."

Sebastian gasped in bitter fury.

"Let me ask you this," Kinley went on. "Do we know that if the South has to give up slavery they will fight to retain it? Yes, we know that. If there is a fight, then it will mean war, and white men will die to set colored folks free. Do you realize what an increase in anti-Negro feeling there would be here in the North? Do you realize that our own lives in Boston would probably be worth very little? Already, as my young friend was reminding us, there have been rumbles of unhappiness from white people here in our city. In a war situation, the whites would attack us day and night."

"We'd hit 'em right back," somebody in the audience called out.

"No, my friends, I say to you that as much as we deplore the peculiar institution called slavery, we must let the South handle its own affairs. Ladies and gentlemen, I thank you for having listened to me."

170

There was applause for him. Sebastian stood up to speak, and the audience coughed and whispered and moved their feet without getting up. The more he tried to sound convincing, the more he found himself groping for words. The crowd was becoming impatient.

There was a murmur outside and Sebastian was almost grateful for the interruption. An usher who had been watching him balefully stepped outside to find out what had caused the trouble. Relieved from sight of those baleful eyes, Sebastian was picking up steam when the usher came back and planted his feet wide apart in the middle of the aisle.

"Whites are coming," he shouted. "Them dockers are going to smash us to pieces for even talking about slavery, just like they said they would. They're down the hill now, all of them carrying big signs and clubs. They heard about this talk, for sure."

Sebastian glanced triumphantly at Squires. "Slavery concerns you now, Squires, like it or not. And you can't get away either, because they're too close. The world has caught up with you. Slavery concerns you and all of us no matter how we feel about it or what we may think about it to ourselves. The world will not retreat in the face of pure reason and faultless selfish logic."

Sebastian had the feeling that it was these next few minutes that his life had been building up to. In a way, too, he would be making it up to the slaves of Rootstock, making it up to them for having done so little of importance during their insurrection. Maybe he had been permitted to remain alive so that he could do other things of importance, like the thing he was going to do now.

He raised the nearby wooden lectern. He unscrewed the top and bottom, leaving himself with a pole that could be used as a club. Then he raised his voice triumphantly.

"We'll all have to meet the whites head-on, and I

want to be in the front line." Carefully, he walked down into the audience and started up the aisle, not looking to his right or left. "I'll do this alone if nobody is with me. Well, friends? Is anybody ready to go out there at my side?"